Love

in the

Valley

A Novella

Love in the Valley

in the

A Novella

LORIN GRACE

CURRANT
CREEK PRESS

Cache Valley

I love this Place.

One

MOTHER'S SUGGESTION OF SLEEPING ON the train was as use-less as the idea of preparing my lessons for the first day of school on the swaying, noisy conveyance. With each new mile the train took me away from my familiar Salt Lake City, my anticipation grew. Each unfamiliar mountain rose higher than those before, looming over towns I'd heard of but never seen. I wondered how the train would make it over them and into the valley where I was to teach school, armed only with my teaching certificate and half a trunk of books.

Past tall mountains, the train followed the tracks to a hill. With a whistle, the train started a trek upward. The train whistle blew again as it crested the long climb. I had my first look at my new home for the next eight months.

I wished for a cleaner window, an impossibility with the soot from the steam engine. Early afternoon sun lit the valley. As near as I could tell, the valley had no lake. According to the maps, there was some marsh land in the center of the valley, but nothing like the Great Salt Lake I was used to. Farms and sage brush as tall as a man dotted the landscape. On the far side of the valley, buildings stood in clumps like the grazing cattle who ignored the train's passing.

The train wouldn't arrive in Logan for nearly an hour as it had stops to make around the edge of the valley. Mendon was larger than I expected. Which, after my siblings teasing about me going to the ends of the earth, was a pleasant surprise. I studied the landscape as we entered Logan. Again, this town was larger and more refined than I expected. One couldn't miss the giant temple on the hill completed just six years earlier. Well-built homes and businesses lined the streets.

The train slowed, and the conductor called out, "Logan station!" Though the school I would teach at was another five miles north, the letter from the school board had instructed me to disembark here rather than to continue to Hyde Park. I tucked a book that I had hardly opened into my carpet bag and smoothed my hair. It didn't feel mussed, so I pinned my hat in place and dusted off my dress, glad that it appeared as tidy as when I'd left Salt Lake early that morning. First impressions mattered, and I didn't want the school board to think I was frumpy. I was not beautiful like my sisters, but in my dark blue skirt and jacket, I looked the part of a smart woman. For once, my plain brown hair and spectacles were to my advantage. As a teacher, looking smart was all that mattered; even if I had wanted to be courted, it was strictly forbidden by my contract.

A great cloud of steam rose when the train stopped. As I followed the other passengers out of the car, I told myself the cessation of the train's movement caused the quaking I felt inside. Most of my fellow passengers vacated the platform. A man in a brown suit checked his pocket watch. Assuming he was waiting for me, I turned in his direction. When I was five feet from him, another man came up and slapped him on his back and they left. I spun, looking for someone else. My trunk sat with a half dozen others at the end of the platform. Laden with books, it was too heavy for me to drag any distance, especially the five miles to the school.

"Miss Hardy?" The question came from a man dressed in a work shirt and much younger than I expected for a school superintendent. I doubted he was old enough to even have a child in a short dress yet. "Are you Miss Jerusha Hardy?"

I bobbed my head before I remembered I should act professional. "Yes, I am."

"My father asked me to fetch you. I'm sorry that I'm late. "

"No bother, Mr.—?"

"Skidmore, Ammon Skidmore." He extended his hand and then pulled it back before he touched my gloved one, as if he was unsure what to do. "Um, do you have a trunk?"

I turned to the pile of trunks. Mine stood alone on the far end. "That is mine, the one with the blue ribbon tied to the top. My brothers said to warn anyone who picked me up that it's heavy. I'm afraid I packed more books than clothes."

"I guess that is good for a teacher to do. My father has been busy gathering readers for the students and everything else to put together a school on short notice. You may find your books are more valuable than your clothes."

I tried not to stare as he hefted the trunk, his muscles rippling under his shirt. I followed him to a wagon where he secured my trunk. He was taller than my oldest brother, which meant he was at least six feet, and the way he threw my trunk as if it were packed with nothing more than summer linens, he had to be the strongest man I'd ever met. That morning, two of my brothers had complained as they loaded my trunk. Mr. Skidmore wasn't even out of breath.

He dusted off the bench seat before handing me up. "There is a square of oilcloth under the seat if you want to cover your skirt. It will be a dusty drive. We haven't had rain in more than two weeks."

The cloth wouldn't protect my jacket or hat, and I was so hot, I couldn't stand the thought of another layer over my clothing. I mumbled a thank you and left the oil cloth were it was.

There were more businesses and houses than I expected. With such differing reports of the valley, I hadn't been sure if I should expect bears and Indians or a town; I was relieved to find it was the latter.

"Ever been to the valley before?"

Ammon's voice was deep.

Did he sing bass? I imagined his voice in harmony with my brothers,' but stopped myself. He might not even sing. Not all families were like mine. Mother sang constantly, a habit that most of my thirteen siblings and I had picked up. Our home was rarely silent.

"No, but my uncle came for the laying of the Temple cornerstones to record the proceedings. He liked the area. I didn't expect the Temple to be pink." I spoke too much, volunteered unasked details, as I did anytime I was nervous. I shouldn't criticize the temple, but the color was definitely not white or gray.

"When they painted the temple, it was supposed to be off white. I like the color of the natural stone better."

"Maybe they meant it to be the same color as the Salt Lake Temple." I had no idea what to say to him. Pink had to be a mistake.

Mr. Skidmore pointed to the canyon just north of us. "That's Green Canyon. Most of the stone came from there, or a canyon in Franklin."

We sat in an uncomfortable silence, as I tried to form a new question. "What do you do, Mr. Skidmore?"

He paused a moment before answering. "You might as well call me Ammon since my father is on the school board and the school is on his land. I am a builder and a farmer. Not sure which one comes first."

The buildings around thinned, and we passed one farm, then another. The road grew dusty. I pulled the oil cloth out and settled it over my skirt, knowing it would be easier to clean later. At a crossroad, Ammon turned east and headed toward the canyon. Trees grew beside cabins, barns, and homes. Few trees grew elsewhere.

"This is the area we call Greenville. Someday we'll start our own town." Ammon turned on a lesser used road, one little more than a dirt track. He pointed to a two-story wood house painted white with green shutters. "That is my father's new house."

A few minutes later, he passed a small log cabin. "This is my father's old house, your school. You'll be boarding with my grand-mother." Ammon nodded at the cabin three hundred yards further, protected by a row of small pines.

Ammon stopped in front of the second cabin. The wood was weathered, yet the small house seemed to be in good repair. A short woman opened the door. A thin gray braid fell over her shoulder. Ammon hopped down and gave the woman a bear hug, leaving me in the wagon. Assuming this was my destination, I did my best to climb out of the high wagon. My straight skirt hindered my progress; reaching the wheel spoke wasn't possible without either exposing half of my leg or ripping the skirt.

Strong hands circled my waist and lifted me to the ground. A shock of awareness jolted through me. Ammon dropped his hands and stepped back. I whirled to face him. He should have asked, especially before grabbing me from behind. I was well aware of what other part of my anatomy was near his face, as it sat just below my waist where I could still feel the warmth of his hands. If I'd worn a bustle, he wouldn't have been able to touch me. I opened my mouth to scold him.

Ammon spoke first. "Sorry, Miss Hardy. I didn't think you'd try to get down without assistance. I should have—" His face reddened, and his grandmother cleared her throat. So, he wasn't completely devoid of manners.

"Welcome, Miss Hardy." The top of the older woman's head didn't even reach my shoulder. She stooped a bit but didn't need the assistance of a cane. She must have been at least seventy, if not older. The three of us were an odd trio as the top of my hat barely reached Ammon's chin. "Shake the dust off and come

5

in. I told Joseph to send the buggy for you, but his wife…" She turned and led me into her cabin.

I left Ammon to get my trunk.

The house was smaller than the kitchen of my mother's home. In one corner sat a stove. The kettle on top took up most of the cooking area. In the other corner below a half loft was a dresser and a bed. A curtain hanging from the loft had been tied back. A small table with two straight-backed chairs and a rocking chair filled the rest of the space. Was I to sleep with the grandmother? Where would I put my dresses?

Ammon came in with my trunk. If he set it down, there would be no space for the three of us to move. With a thump, he left it outside the open doorway. "Before I take this up to the loft, are there any books or things you want out?"

The loft ran the entire length of the cabin and was five feet wide. Standing on my tip toes, I could just see the end of a narrow bed. How was he to get a large trunk up the ladder? How would I not fall off the edge trying to get dressed? I hadn't needed the semester of science to know that Isaac Newton's theory of gravity was real. If there was a rock to trip over, I would find it. Giving me a ladder and a loft was a guarantee I'd break my neck before Christmas.

Before I could answer, his grandmother spoke. "Ammon, before you take that up, will you take up the tick? It's out back. I filled it with fresh straw."

Apparently, I was to have my own room or loft. I was glad I had brought two more serviceable skirts along; I would never be able to climb the ladder in this dress with any degree of modesty or in the other narrow ones I brought to teach in. Or my bustle. I'd worry about that later, providing I didn't fall out of the loft to begin with.

Unloading the books depleted half my trunk. I stacked them neatly against the wall. I hadn't thought I'd managed so many with my dresses and winter clothing. I closed the lid before Ammon could see the white lace of my underthings. He swung my light-ened trunk up with such force that he hoisted it over the edge of the loft without climbing the ladder.

"Do you need anything else?" Ammon addressed his grand-mother.

"Are you staying for supper?"

"Do you have enough?"

"The garden and the chickens are producing faster than I can eat right now. I pickled tomatoes yesterday, and my cellar is almost full. Nothing fancy, just boiled eggs, vegetables, and bread." His grandmother uncovered a crock in her small cupboard.

Ammon nodded and left the cabin. He unhitched the horses and led them around the house.

I realized I had two problems. One, I still didn't know my host-ess's name, and two, was I supposed to pay her or did the school board? There were only two chairs. Maybe I wasn't supposed to eat here at all.

"I put water in a pitcher up in your loft. If you hurry, you can wash up and get that jacket off before he comes back in. No need to dress like that in this heat."

I made it up the ladder without falling. No siblings applauded my accomplishment. The valley was a long way from home.

After dinner, I was still no wiser as to what to call my hostess. There had been a long discussion between Ammon and his grand-mother. It didn't take me long to realize that Ammon's mother had passed and that his father had remarried. This grandmother was his maternal one. Some of my students would be his half siblings. Oddly, whenever either of them brought up the current Mrs. Skidmore, they often left a sentence unfinished. I assumed Ammon didn't get on well with his stepmother.

Ammon admonished his grandmother to tell him if she didn't get paid by his father for my room and board. I didn't ask any details; I hoped what they offered was adequate even for so small a place. It was better than moving from house to house every few weeks as many rural teachers did.

"Go show her the schoolhouse." His grandmother shooed us out of the cabin before I could clear our dishes from the table. Wordlessly, Ammon hefted the larger pile of books. I grabbed the smaller pile and followed him out the door.

The schoolhouse was smaller than the cabin we just left. I tried to hide my shock. A family once lived here? Where had they slept?

I'd never been in a one-room schoolhouse before, and I pictured rows of students facing the teacher as I had when I went to school. A single window faced north. Evening shadow cloaked the room. I set my books on the small desk in the front center of the room. The walls to my left and right were lined with a long table attached to the wall between the chinking of the logs. A newly built bench sat under each table, leaving the center of the room open. The letter I had received indicated I was to have 15 fifteen students. Unless they were very small, there wouldn't be room for them at the tables. If the students faced their desk or table, I would be teaching to their backs. And half the children would be looking out the single window.

"Well?" He drew out the single word into a longer question.

"It's clean."

"And?"

"Different from I expected. I thought there would be desks facing the front of the room. The blackboard looks new." I opened the desk drawer. Chalk, pencils, and paper sat divided by thin spacers. The desk was dented and scratched.

"Both schools I went to had desks facing the front too. Dad said nailing the table to the wall saved on lumber."

"Both schools?"

"We lived in Salt Lake until I was thirteen. I went back down to take classes at the University of Deseret. Dad wanted me to go to college in the East, but there wasn't enough money for me to go, too." Ammon shrugged. "I wanted to be a farmer anyway."

Mama warned me about judging people. I'd never guessed that Ammon had gone to school beyond the basics. I didn't pry further. "I'm not sure how to teach with everyone looking at the wall or out the window."

"You'll teach in small groups anyway. If you had a bench in front of your desk, the ones you are teaching could sit and face you."

"Where might I purchase a bench?"

Ammon laughed. I hadn't seen a furniture store, but there must be one in Logan. It wasn't that backwards.

"I can make you a simple bench before Monday morning."

"How much?" The school had to have a budget. At least I hoped they did. My pay wasn't half of what my sister made two years ago in Provo.

Ammon crossed his arms and considered me. I had the urge to smooth my skirts. "A Saturday's labor."

"I'm not skilled at much."

"Apple picking. A week from tomorrow. I'll need all the help I can get."

"Do I have to climb a ladder?"

"No. Are you scared of heights?"

The room was in enough shadow now, I hoped he couldn't see my face. "Not exactly. Ladders have a way of tipping over when I am on them."

"You can stay on the ground."

I agreed and locked the school behind us. Ammon walked me back to his grandmother's. She sat out on the porch. I needed to ask her name.

Ammon left me and walked to the stable to the west of the house.

"Was the school everything you expected?" asked his grandma.

"It was different, but I'll get along." I leaned against one of the posts that supported the roof over the porch. "I should have asked hours ago… What is your name?"

She laughed. "I wondered how long you would go without asking. I should have introduced myself. Emeline Wood. Most people call me Widow Wood or Sister Wood. Since we are going to know everything about each other, call me Em. No one has called me that for years."

I hesitated. She was four times my age.

"Or you can call me Grandma."

"Grandma Em?"

Ammon came back around the house with the horses and hitched them to the wagon. He hugged Grandma Em. "I'll be here Sunday morning to take you to church. You too, Miss Hardy."

I returned his nod.

Grandma Em lit the cabin with a single lantern, leaving most of the loft in deep shadow. I stayed as far away as possible from the edge as I dressed for bed. The water in the pitcher was warm but welcome in removing the dust that managed to sneak under my clothes. Grandma Em called up before extinguishing the lamp.

I'd never slept on a bed filled with straw. It was more comfortable that I thought. A faint smell of lavender teased my nose. I sniffed at my bedding and decided Grandma Em must have added dried flowers to my bedding. The lavender made my dreams sweeter than I expected.

Two

Monday morning, I arrived at the school an hour before I would ring the bell standing on a post in the schoolyard. A three-foot-long bench sat next to the door. I dragged it inside. My fashionably straight skirt and bustle hindered my movements. No wonder so many of the women wore fuller ones to church yesterday.

A boy of eight or so arrived ten minutes later. He stood outside and watched me through the window. I opened it. "Welcome. You can come in."

He shook his head and stepped back. I sat at my desk and reviewed my plan for the day. Soon more children joined the boy. I expected they would either come in or play. Instead, all of them watched me through the window as if waiting for me to give the opening lines to a play. I checked my watch. Twenty-three minutes left until I rang the bell at nine. Instead of being calmed by my preparation time, my nerves grew with each passing minute. A sudden urge to visit the outhouse swept through me as it did whenever I was nervous. I'd heard of pranks pulled on new teachers by students: frogs in desks, snakes in lunch pails, and worst of all, being tied in the outhouse or having it tipped on its side.

Fifteen minutes until I rang the morning bell. Calmly, I walked out of the school and locked the door. I greeted the silent children, then hurried up the road to use Grandma Em's outhouse. None of the children would dare tie me in there.

Em looked up from her garden. "Is something wrong? School starts soon."

"I just needed to use the privy."

"Why not use the school's?"

I opened the outhouse door. "What if they tie me inside?"

I was prepared for Grandma Em's laugh but not for Ammon's guffaw. I spun to see him at the other end of the garden leading an ox. Mortified, I stepped into the privy and let the door slam behind me.

On my way back to the school, I didn't look to see where Ammon was. I arrived back with three minutes to spare. Thirteen of my fifteen students stood around the schoolyard. I unlocked the schoolroom and took off my hat. I had just enough time to take a deep breath before returning outside and ringing the bell. The older children lined up in two lines, boys and girls. They herded the younger ones, including one who looked to be only three or four, into the lines with them. They followed me into the school. Again, the older students showed the younger what to do. I assumed most of them had been in a school before.

"Good morning, students."

"Good morning, Miss Hardy."

I led them through the song and the scripture of the day, which I'd written on the board Saturday when I'd prepared the room. Three of my students were Skidmores, but unlike their older half-brother, they were all blonds. The oldest student was Mary Flick. At almost fifteen, I wondered why she was here instead of at Brigham Young College in Logan. According to the children, the three missing boys were still helping with harvest. As I suspected, the youngest student wasn't supposed to be in school yet. She was another Skidmore. I asked the oldest brother, Nathan, to take her home.

"I can't. Ma went into town and said Sally had to stay with us."

I gave Sally a slate and chalk and let her sit with her brother. We spent the rest of the morning doing arithmetic drills. As I suspected, Mary had more than mastered the curriculum I had prepared, but she stuttered whenever I called on her. Previous teachers must have equated the stutter with ignorance.

I called a lunch break just before noon and asked Nathan to take his sister home. All the Skidmore children left, which was not surprising as their house was less than a quarter mile way. The other children scattered into groups around the schoolyard in the shade of the young trees. The younger boys played tag.

An hour later, I rang the bell. The Skidmore children had not returned. For the spelling bee, I asked the children to write on their slates. I wanted to know how well Mary could spell, and her stutter would make that impossible. One of the older girls complained that spelling bees were not supposed to be written.

A half hour later, the Skidmore children returned with Mrs. Skidmore, Sally balanced on her hip. They marched into the classroom, stopping our lesson. Mrs. Skidmore pushed Sally to the front of my desk.

"Nathan says you won't let Sally stay at school."

The students stared at us.

"Children, pull out your readers and turn to the last story you read. Mary, will you help the younger ones write out their alphabets? Mrs. Skidmore and I will be right outside."

Mrs. Skidmore left the room, but at a nod to Nathan she left Sally there. I took Sally by the hand and led her out after her mother.

"Sally needs to stay at school."

A dozen solutions ran through my brain. I could not let Mrs. Skidmore flaunt the regulations, even if her husband was the superintendent. "She is too young, and you are interrupting my classroom. School ends at three. Come back then."

"Well, I never…"

I turned my back on her and returned to the classroom. Despite the heat, I shut the door, sending the message that she wasn't welcome.

Each student read a passage to me from their reader. Mary struggled over hers, and I found myself glaring at most of the older boys to control their snickering. I needed to have a private conversation with Mary. From the novel she hid in her lunch pail, I suspected she read at a higher level than her reader. By the end of the day, I confirmed most of their levels and switched the seating order. Pricilla, the one who complained about the spelling bee, was miffed to have to trade with Mary. However, Mary's math calculations and written spelling showed she had the higher proficiency.

I sent the students home with reading assignments at three o'clock. Five minutes later, Mr. Skidmore entered the classroom.

"My wife says you were rude to her."

I'd met the superintendent at church. In his late sixties, he was twice the age of his wife. Not all that uncommon. The widower who had wanted to marry me was three times my age.

"Mrs. Skidmore sent your three-year-old daughter to school. Then she brought the three children here back a half hour late from lunch and disrupted my classroom." Being one of the younger children in my family, I defended my position first and asked if it was worth defending later.

"So, you were rude to her?" He stood in front of my desk and glared down at me.

"I told her to return after school to discuss matters."

"I will not tolerate rudeness to my wife."

Using my calmest voice, I attempted to explain. "I didn't mean to be rude. I had twelve students sitting in the classroom alone."

He crossed his arms. "I require an apology."

My jaw clenched. Standing my ground might mean I would be out on the next train. I wouldn't fail after only one day. "I will give her one. Now about Sally, she simply cannot attend school."

"She sent Sally?"

Had he not been listening to me? "Yes."

"Sally is too young to be here."

At least we agreed on that point.

"My wife must have had a good reason."

"Reason or not, Sally is too young. What if the other seven families sent their little ones to school? Teaching would be impossible."

"Did Sally disturb class this morning?" He stepped back from my desk.

I stood so I could look him in the eye. "I don't think that is the point. The guidelines you sent me are clear. She doesn't belong here."

"It would happen only a few times. My wife goes into Logan to help her sister on occasion." His excuse fell hollow on my ears.

"Mr. Skidmore, as the superintendent, you can't ask me to violate policy. The school inspector could come any day."

For a moment, I thought he would agree. "But my wife…"

Things Ammon and Grandma Em hadn't said formed into assumptions. Mr. Skidmore was more afraid of his wife than he was of school guidelines. "I'm truly sorry, Mr. Skidmore. When I signed my contract, I agreed to several policies including the district guidelines. I can write the inspector for permission, but without his approval she cannot come to class."

Mr. Skidmore stepped back. "No, no, don't write him. I'll find another solution."

"Is there anything else?"

"My wife told me you left the school this morning with all the children in the schoolyard. Is that true?"

"I did."

"That is unacceptable."

"I left at a quarter till eight. School was not yet in session. I returned before the hour and started school on time. I was unaware I needed to be here earlier than my contract stated."

He blustered for a moment. "Well, then. See that you don't leave them unattended during class hours."

Mr. Skidmore left. Had the meeting left him as dissatisfied as it had me? The uncomfortable feeling that I may have won the first battle of a long war filled my heart with dread.

Each morning I checked the drawers of my desk. Still no rodents or reptiles. Did this mean my students liked me or feared me? I'd heard so many stories about pranks students played on teachers and had witnessed a few initiated by one or another of my brothers.

Over the next four days, Mrs. Skidmore clearly defined the lines for the next battle. Every day, one or more of the Skidmore children were late to school or returning from lunch hour. The excuse was always the same, "Mother needed help." I wished I could give Mrs. Skidmore lines to copy out of the fifth reader for causing her children to be tardy. I wasn't sure what the policy was on tardiness, so I had the tardy children make up their lessons after school which only resulted in the children being later the following day. I needed a solution that wouldn't make them soldiers in their mother's war with me. I tried to focus on the rest of my students, although the Skidmore issue was never far from my mind.

I loaned Mary my copy of Jane Austen's *Emma* and asked her to write a report on the novel. I also administered an advanced arithmetic test to her. As I suspected, her knowledge eclipsed mine. The dismal marks sent from last year's school told another story. I suspected the teachers dismissed her because of the stutter. Since most lessons were recited from memory, her stutter made it impossible to articulate her knowledge. I resolved to meet her parents as well as the parents of my other students. I'd start next week when I knew the children better.

Each night, Grandma Em asked me about my day. I never mentioned the Skidmores. I figured it was too close to family and crossed the lines. I told her how little David Baker came early each morning to school so he could read ahead in his reader to catch up with his sister. Grandma Em laughed at my fears of having a mouse or snake in my desk, pointing out that the parents had worked hard to get the school open and none of the children wanted to face punishment at home for scaring the teacher. After that, I used the school outhouse during the lunch hour without fear of being tied in or it being tipped over.

In the evenings, I helped around the house as much as I could. We had chickens at home, so I volunteered to take care of Grandma Em's hens. I avoided the goat as much as possible.

Each day Ammon passed by the school on his way to Em's. I assumed he took care of the goats and brought down water from the spring or canal as Em's place didn't have a well and the hogshead rain barrel stood empty waiting for rain. I didn't ask about him; as a teacher, romantic relationships where not permitted, and at my age, friendships with men either ended in marriage or heartbreak. I had sisters enough to prove that theory. Unfortunately, I couldn't keep from thinking about him more than I should. He was one of the most handsome men I ever met, and so far, had only treated me with kindness.

Oddly enough, my biggest obstacle each day was the railless loft. I was sure I would topple over the edge. I learned to dress sitting on my bed and avoided going up during the day when Grandma would see me crawl across the floor to the bed's safety. I'd tied an old sash to the corner of the bed frame as soon as I was up the ladder and cling to it until I reached the bed. Refilling my water pitcher each day filled me with dread. I was sure I would fall off the ladder with only one arm to balance going up and coming down. However, I was so grateful I didn't have to move from house to house each week like my cousin had when she taught out in Tooele that I had no intention to complain. All in all, I considered my first week a success.

Friday, after entering the children's grades in the book, I returned to Em's, finding Ammon's wagon sitting in the yard. The ringing of a hammer came from inside of the cabin.

"The bottom rope is sagging." Em stood in the doorway, hands on her hips with her back to me. Over her shoulder, I saw Ammon in my loft. He'd built a rope and post balustrade, which looked more like a three-rung fence along the entire length of the loft. They had moved the ladder from the center of the room to the wall, only the angle more closely resembled stairs than a ladder. It too had a rope railing.

Grandma turned to greet me. "We hoped to have this done before you returned. You should have told me heights bothered you last week instead of crawling on your hands and knees."

Heat filled my cheeks. I wanted no one to know of my silly fear. "It isn't the height. At home we have stairs almost twice as high. It's falling. I trip over my own feet on a regular basis. If I fell up there…" I let the thought trail off.

Ammon knelt in the loft. "Now you won't need to crawl around up here."

Grandma Em gave him a scolding look.

I couldn't meet either of their eyes as I answered. "Thank you. I'll worry much less about tripping over the edge."

Ammon tightened the rope threaded through the posts. "I should have thought about this years ago. Once or twice, I almost came over the edge."

"You used to live here?"

Ammon and Grandma Em exchanged a look. He rubbed the back of his neck. "Grandma raised me after my mother died. I just moved into my new place this summer."

"But it isn't finished yet." One topic Grandma Em never failed to discuss was the stone home Ammon was building or how nice his new barn was.

"The barn and cellar are, and I should have the walls two feet higher before the first snow." Ammon gave me a half smile as if I hadn't taken his place in a warm house.

"You left because of me?"

Grandma Em patted my hand. "No, child, he moved out in the spring. With his barn finished, it was more efficient to stay there."

"But this winter?" There was no reason I couldn't room with other families.

"I'll be as warm as a bear in his den." Ammon took his tools to the wagon.

"Grandma Em, you didn't need to rearrange the entire house for me."

"I never liked the ladder in the middle of the room."

What was done was done. I tested out the new stairs. My skirt didn't get tangled once.

Ammon returned. "You're still coming to pick apples tomorrow?"

"Of course. That bench is perfect. I mean, even if it wasn't, I'd come."

"See you in the morning." He settled his hat on his head as he left the cabin.

"Thank you for the stairs and railing." I called as he walked away. Now, all I needed was a way to hang a quilt or something so I could change clothes in the middle of the day. When I returned to Salt Lake, I'd never complain about sharing a room with my sisters again.

Three

THE APPLE TREES WERE SHORTER than I expected. According to Ammon, they were only five years old, and this was their first big harvest.

Nathan Skidmore traded my full basket with an empty one. "Miss Hardy."

I returned his acknowledgment. A dozen people harvested other trees. Grandma Em picked three bushels herself before the sun was high overhead. A woman with a child holding her skirt carried a bucket of water. I deposited my apronful of apples in a basket and stretched my back.

She handed me the dipper. "I'm Cornella Skidmore, Moroni's wife."

"Nice to meet you. I'm Jerusha Hardy, the new schoolteacher."

"You're staying with Grandma Wood?"

I nodded as I drank from the dipper.

"I've asked Grandma to supper after church. Will you come with her?"

"Yes, thank you." I handed back the dipper.

"Ammon will bring you. Oh, and Moroni is the brother who lives in Hyde Park. It is easy to get them confused."

"Nephi, is the one in St. George, right?" I asked.

"And Joseph is in Logan, and Sariah is in Brigham City."

I nodded. Grandma Em talked often of her grandchildren and the several great-grandchildren, some she'd met and others, like Nephi's children, that she assumed she'd never meet in this lifetime. Someone called Cornella's name, and she moved on. I returned to picking apples and designing practical arithmetic problems based on the numbers of apples it took to fill a bushel basket. Soon, I finished the tree and moved on to one several rows down.

Ammon came with an empty basket.

"May I buy a bushel of apples?" I asked.

"Grandma already has six, including the ones I gave her. Why do you need more?"

"School. I've thought of several math problems from counting the number of apples in a bushel to figuring the yield per orchard. I thought real apples might help them think about more than just numbers."

"I could loan them too you." He picked several apples from the higher branches.

"After a day of children handling them, they'd only be good for applesauce."

"But aren't we supposed to give teachers apples?" His eyes sparkled when he grinned.

I couldn't resist teasing him back. "Only schools who pay the teachers in goods do that. I get paid in cash."

"You could consider it my payment."

"You don't have children in the school." I started filling a new bucket.

"But I want to support the school."

"So far, you picked me up from the station, built me a railing for the loft, and built me a bench for the schoolroom. You're more than helping."

He filled another basket. "I don't feel right about you buying the apples for a school lesson."

I didn't feel right about him giving them to me either. Mostly because I knew I was thinking of him too often. I still had one hundred and twenty-five school days left in my teaching contract. I shouldn't be thinking of any man at all. Arguing with him felt too close to flirtation. "Then I thank you for another donation to the school."

"How was your first week?"

"Better than I expected. The children are bright, and I found no snakes in my drawer." I hoped he wouldn't bring up my trip to Em's outhouse.

Ammon smiled. "I only remember one boy doing anything like that to a teacher when I went to school. You're probably safe."

"I must seem like a little bundle of fears to you—mice, snakes, the loft."

"The loft was a reasonable fear. I did come close to falling off a time or two. Especially when Nephi and I got to wrestling."

I'd watched my own brothers go at it many times. I shuddered at the thought of boys falling. "Poor Grandma Em."

"Poor us. She'd make gingerbread or apple tarts and only give them to Sariah and Moroni." Ammon ducked his head in an effort to look contrite.

"What of Joseph Junior?

"He lived with Pa or was away at school. As soon as he left, Moroni took his place."

"You lived in the school, right?"

"Yes, there was a loft in there that we closed off this summer. Didn't want the kids climbing up there and throwing things on the teacher." Ammon tossed a handful of leaves at me, and I jumped.

"I thought you said I'd be safe from pranks."

"Some boys think the teacher is pretty and just want her attention." His rich laughter echoed through the trees as he moved on to help the next person.

I pulled a leaf from my hair. He had my attention.

Monday morning during our arithmetic lesson, as the younger children counted the apples, an incessant squeaking filled the room. At first, I thought it was one of the boys. Unfortunately, it was a sound I'd heard before: mice. Newborn mice, to be specific. The children recognized it too. After several minutes, I stopped the lesson as everyone was trying to find the source of the squeaking. Nathan located the new family inside of the potbelly stove. He removed them using the ash pail. Class resumed with my lesson only partially interrupted.

When arithmetic concluded, I rewarded all the children with an apple at lunchtime. A reward more calculated to rid myself of apples as Grandma Em already had more than enough to dry. I used my lunch hour to take the rest of the apples to Em and tell her about the mice.

The Skidmore children didn't return on time after lunch, again. I pulled out my copy of Robinson Crusoe and began to read. I read for twenty minutes until the Skidmores arrived, finishing a page as they sat down. Missing the story would be punishment enough for the children, since I suspected their mother was the cause of the extended lunches, and it solved my problem with how to handle the extra time.

I asked the second reader group up to the bench, and I opened my desk drawer to get—

The mouse landed on my skirt.

Several of the girls screamed.

I shook the rodent off and watched with wide eyes as he ran down the center of the room. The boys chased him out the door.

When things were calm, I searched each of the students' faces. "I will not ask who put the mouse in my desk since I don't want anyone to lie or bear false witness. Perhaps we would be all served by reversing our five-finger lesson."

I held up my thumb and pointed to it. The students repeated the need to be truthful. We all pointed to our forefingers representing honesty. We followed with punctuality, cleanliness, and ending with our pinky finger of kindness.

"While I am working with the reading groups, those not reading will write about one of those five principles or copy that lesson from your readers to your slates."

The remainder of the day passed without incident.

As I closed the school, Mrs. Skidmore came into the schoolyard. "My children said you read a story to the rest of the students but not to them."

"Yes, I have started reading a book after lunch. All those who return on time will participate."

"So, you are punishing my children because they are late?"

"No, I am rewarding those who are on time. I am allowed to punish them if they are late, but I don't believe having them stand in a corner, write lines, or receive lashes will solve their tardiness."

"But they need to care for Sally while I rest." She crossed her arms.

"Then they will miss the story."

"That isn't fair to my children."

"Others who leave school return on time." I walked around the room, straightening it.

Mrs. Skidmore blocked my path. "Mine can't. Move reading time."

"Reading time is after lunch."

"My children will miss the book."

"Better than missing lessons. If you want your children to participate, send them back to school before I ring the bell." The roof of the Skidmore house was visible from the door of the school. If she sent them back to school when the bell rang, they could run and still be on time.

Mrs. Skidmore's mouth hung open for a moment. "You are a very impertinent girl."

"No, ma'am, I'm a teacher. Do you have any more questions? I am on my way to an appointment." A twinge of guilt twisted in the back of my mind. I shouldn't treat any of the students' parents with disrespect, even if they were the problem.

"Mr. Skidmore will hear of this."

"Maybe he will have a solution for your children's constant tardiness." I knew I shouldn't have spoken my mind so freely. I opened my pin watch. I hadn't set an exact time for my first home visit, but the house was about a mile away. "Have a good day, Mrs. Skidmore."

Unfortunately, I needed to walk in the direction of the Skidmores to reach my destination. I decided to take my extra books back to Em's, thus avoiding walking with Mrs. Skidmore.

Ammon unloaded a box of dry goods from the back of his wagon. "How was your apple lesson?"

"It went very well. The younger children seemed to understand the connection between the single apple and what a wagonload might bring when sold. Far better than when we just use numbers."

"I just returned from taking a load to the station. I wonder if I received enough money?"

"I don't know, I only sold them for fifteen cents a bushel." My price was deliberately low. Ammon had the only orchard for miles, and I didn't want the children thinking about what he made as many of them came by to pick apples for their families.

"Good thing I sold them by the barrel. Your prices would bankrupt me."

"Even with the free labor?"

Ammon laughed. "Everyone was either paid in apples or something else I bartered."

"Oh, I left your basket at the school. I was going to return it this afternoon on my way to the Flick's farm." I wanted to meet with Mary's family first. I hoped her parents would welcome the news that I believed her prior marks were much lower than they should have been.

"Would you like a ride?"

"Won't that take you out of your way?" I wanted to spend time with him more than I should.

"Not too far."

"It wouldn't be an imposition?"

"Not at all." His grin melted my resistance.

I agreed and hurried inside to deposit my books.

At the schoolhouse, Ammon stayed in the wagon and handed me down to get the basket. There was one bruised apple left in the bottom. Ammon and I joked about what it would be good for during the short ride. The ideas started out mundane, feed to a pig, sauce, bake in a pie. By the time we arrived at the Flicks, we were both laughing at using the apple to catch a fish.

My family meetings went well. Mrs. Flick had been more pleased than Mr. Flick at my analysis of their daughter's skills. His reluctance may have been more about my suggestion that she go to Brigham Young College than her about her previous marks. Other families asked me to stay for dinner or a slice of pie.

Mr. Skidmore stopped into my school—technically his—late the following Thursday. "I have had reports that you are not acting in compliance with your contract and have been stepping out with a young man."

I'd expected something about his children, not about me. My mind raced before answering. "Then you've received false reports."

"You were seen holding hands in front of this very school." He stood in front of my desk and glared down at me.

I pushed back from the desk so I didn't need to strain to look at him. "I haven't held anyone's hand, other than the children's when we've played games, and then only the youngest ones.'"

"I have my information from a reliable source. And I know for a fact you often talk to the young man."

I closed my grading ledger. Suspicion filled me. There was only one man I spoke with regularly, and I had been circumspect in all my dealings with him. "To whom do you refer?"

"My son, Ammon."

I thought back over each touch I shared with Ammon. Surprised how my mind had cataloged even the most innocent of them. "The only times that I have held your son's hand, so to speak, is when he has handed me down from a wagon."

"You were laughing with him."

Laughing was not in the rules of my contract. "Your son has a sense of humor, so I laughed."

Mr. Skidmore frowned. "You are starting rumors."

"I am not the one gossiping about other people." As soon as the words were out of my mouth, I regretted them. Mrs. Skidmore or the children were the only people likely to have seen us at the schoolhouse that day.

"See that you be more careful, and stay away from my son. He is not meant for you. Don't make me remind you of the rules again, Miss Hardy, or you'll be without a job. You are here to teach, not to find a husband." He slammed the schoolhouse door, rattling the window as he left.

The desire to throw the bruised apple that a student left for me that morning at the superintendent's retreating back filled me .

I was well aware of my inability to court while I taught. Female teachers were expected to stay single. Some did get engaged, but not without some measure of scandal. A married woman might teach the basics of reading and arithmetic to a few children in her own home, but that was not the same as being a teacher for a school.

Courting had been the furthest thing from my mind when I took the job. I told Father I wasn't ready to marry. Which was a partial truth. I wasn't ready to marry the widower Mr. King, whose seven children needed a mother—which I was not ready to be. I was scarcely four years older than the King's oldest son.

Only one month of teaching had shown me that I didn't have the patience to deal with seven children every moment of the day. It might be different if they were my own and they weren't taller than me to start with.

Ammon. There was no other recourse than to avoid him. I couldn't deny that I enjoyed his conversation, and the better I came to know him, the more I admired him. The few times he had touched me, I had felt his touch burn me to my core… My older sisters had spoken of such things during their courting. Even Hannah, who became Brother Weld's third wife, said she felt such a thing. I longed for my sisters' advice, but putting my questions into words would be admitting that my heart was having difficulty with the rules put upon me by the school board. Which only two weeks into teaching would have me fired by Christmas. Besides, Ammon's father clearly had someone in mind other than a teacher from outside of the valley.

I opened my ledger and finished entering the day's marks. The sun was setting over the western mountains by the time I walked to Em's. I stayed at the school longer than I needed to so I wouldn't run into Ammon if he happened to be around. My plan didn't work. His buckboard was parked in front of the cabin. Inside, he sat across from Em at the small table eating dinner.

"Did you visit another family tonight?" Em's query carried the unspoken question of why I didn't tell her I was going to be late.

"Sorry, I had an unexpected visitor at the school, and it put me off schedule." Nothing in that was a lie. "I should have walked home earlier."

"No harm done. Ammon didn't eat all of your portion." As if Em ever made only two portions of anything but breakfast. We had extras more evenings than not, which Em rebaked into stews or pies.

Ammon took his dish and sat in the rocking chair. Neither of them asked me about my visitor, and I didn't elaborate. The conversation centered around the opening of the new agricultural college and the weather. Having no experience with winter in the valley, I offered little to the conversation. Ammon left as soon as he finished. Only after he took his leave did I realize he never spoke directly to me the entire dinner. All of his comments had been to Grandma Em or directed at both us. He must have had an unexpected visitor, too.

Four

OCTOBER BROUGHT COOLER WEATHER—WARM SOME days and freezing the next. I handed out rotations to the older boys for emptying the ashes from the potbelly stove and starting a fire on mornings cold enough to see our breath inside of the school-house. Fortunately, no more mice took up residence. No one ever claimed to be the one to put the mouse in my desk.

The item my classroom lacked was a map. One warm morning while teaching a history lesson, it became clear that the younger children struggled with the concept of an entire world beyond their little valley. They viewed Salt Lake to be just on the other side of the mountains, and beyond that, they were lost. The small illustrations in my old textbook were difficult to see, and when I explained that the valley was no larger than a pinprick, even my older students laughed.

As I dismissed them for the lunch hour, a feeling of defeat settled over me. A larger map or a globe would be so helpful. Even a large ball that I could draw on. I hadn't even tackled explaining that the world was round, a concept that was sure to fail when they lived in a valley shaped like a long, high-edged platter.

Em had packed biscuits and a chicken wing left from Sunday's dinner along with the obligatory apple. If only the apple was as large as a globe. I tossed it up as if it were a ball and caught it before it hit my desk. And there was my answer sitting across the room. Not exactly round, but the potbelly stove would do. The day was warm, so the stove hadn't been lit.

I grabbed a slate pencil and started drawing. There would be no cartography award for my work, and it was not to scale. I continued through the end of the lunch hour. It was David Baker's turn to ring the bell, a reward for moving up to the next reader so quickly. Instead of returning to their seats, the children gathered around where I knelt in front of the stove.

"I need a few more minutes to finish this. Nathan, will you read the next chapter of Robinson Crusoe? And the rest of you, he can only read as long as you sit in your seats." The Skidmore children hadn't missed a chapter of the book since the conversation with their mother, and I hadn't experienced any further visits. I had caught Mrs. Skidmore watching me at church, but she never spoke. I stayed as far from Ammon as possible, not wanting to cause problems for either of us.

I finished outlining China just as Nathan concluded the chapter. I checked my handiwork. Australia was too large and Canada out of proportion. None of my students would be able to correct me, so I dusted off my hands and started the lesson. I didn't anticipate some of the questions.

"Why is there more water than land?"

"Dad came from Wales. Where is that?"

"My dad came on a boat from England. He said it took a month. Is that true?" Several of the children had stories from parents or grandparents that verified this. Some longer.

"How do people stand on the world if it's round?" Gravity was a lesson for another day. I found myself wanting to answer, "Because God made it that way," more than once.

"How long would it take to go around the entire world?"

"What if we took a train around the world?"

I showed them how it wasn't possible to take a train round the world before moving on to arithmetic. I told them how things were moving faster and faster in the world, that an express train could travel from the east coast to the west in only eighty-three hours. Many of their grandparents or parents made a journey only half as long in one hundred days. We discussed how the first settlers in the valley had to travel by wagon several days from Salt Lake. When I came to the valley, I was on the train for only a few hours and made many stops.

"A wagon train only traveled about ten miles a day. A modern train travels at thirty-five miles an hour. How long does it take to go one thousand miles?" Once the upper-grade students found an answer, I had them help the younger students. I took a moment to revise my plans for the day and assigned them pages from their primers for the rest of arithmetic time.

I had the last of my family visits that evening. The one I'd been dreading: the Skidmores. Since their children were doing well, there wasn't much for me to say. Mrs. Skidmore softened some-what during my family visit. Evidently, hearing how well her children fared in school was a boon. She applauded my creativity with the potbellied globe and reminisced about her own teaching days in Pennsylvania before coming west. She, of course, had had the latest in maps and lamented her children didn't have one to learn from.

Mrs. Skidmore was surprisingly kind and offered me a slice of cake. "Do you enjoy teaching? Do you plan on staying?"

"Teaching is enjoyable." I didn't elaborate because the children and Mr. Skidmore listened. "I hadn't thought about next year." My situation was nice enough, but I made my answer vague. "As far as staying on, I can't say I'd considered it, but I also hadn't thought of leaving."

On the way back to Grandma Em's, I pondered my future. As a child, I always assumed I would grow up and marry, but what if my offers only came from men like Mr. King? What if no one ever offered again? After all, as a schoolteacher, I was hardly likely to find myself in a position to marry. The one man I felt I could like enough to even consider marrying was out of my reach precisely because I was the teacher.

When I taught about geology, several of my students mentioned visiting the quarry up Green Canyon where the temple stones had been dug, and their descriptions made me feel adventurous. If I stayed in the valley long-term, I wanted local examples to help the children learn about common minerals. The cloudless November Saturday was as good a day as any to explore. The temple quarry couldn't be that far up the canyon if most of my students had visited it. With the sun setting earlier in the day, I had little time to walk far after the school day ended. I finished my chores early and made a lunch. I took the road east, which wasn't much more than a wagon track leading up the bench to Ammon's farm. Only a trickle of water ran in the canal. Someone had laid three timbers across. The makeshift bridge was wide enough for a horse, judging by the tracks left in the dirt. I found a road running northeast to the mouth of Green Canyon. It must be the road they used to haul the stones across the bench to Logan.

Yellow and orange leaves danced in the breeze, holding on to the few small trees growing near the canyon's mouth. Plumes of dust danced around my feet on the hard-packed road. Moving stone for the temple and other buildings using wagons and sleds had smoothed out the bumps. The ground was so packed I couldn't dent it with my boot heel. I followed the road into the canyon.

The quarry wasn't hard to find, as the canyon was narrow and straight. Three buildings stood near the quarry. From the smoke and smell of fresh bread, one was a cookhouse. A lone wagon stood near a large pile of stone. I recognized Ammon's hat from the distance.

It wouldn't do for him to see me here. If he offered me a ride back down, I'd be obliged to accept just as he was forced to offer.

I had only seen him on Sunday for the last two weeks. Neither Grandma Em nor I mentioned his absence at the cabin, although there was evidence enough that he was there during the day. I was positive that Mr. Skidmore had had the same discussion with Ammon as he had with me, pointing out that I was not good enough to be Ammon's wife. Some measure of kindness existed in his absence as I found it impossible to believe that he entertained any interest in me as anything other than his grandmother's boarder.

I had hoped to collect a small rock from both the red and blue rock quarries for the children to examine and discuss. Since I had yet to borrow or purchase a book on geology, actual minerals were the only material I had to teach them. It took me a moment to realize that Ammon and his team of oxen were walking toward me. With such a large load, the animals would move slowly, just like the slow-moving wagon trains. He would not be obligated to offer me a ride after all. I continued up to the cabin.

"Miss Hardy, what are you doing up here?" Ammon called from several yards away.

I watched the lumbering oxen rather than look him in the face. "I have come to look at the quarries."

"They are dangerous places. Not meant to be gawked at and definitely not a place for a lone woman to explore. You need an escort."

His tone grated on my nerves. "I can take care of myself."

Ammon shook his head. "That isn't what I meant. Some men up here are hired men and not accustomed to a lady's presence. If your father were here, he would not want you around those men unescorted either."

"Thank you for the warning." I walked past him and continued up the canyon. He might be right, but I was in no mood to be told what to do by the man who I was supposed to be keeping my distance from. I hadn't walked ten feet when I heard Ammon's footfalls behind me. He grabbed me by the elbow. "Jerusha— I mean, Miss Hardy—please do not go up there. I'll take you myself another day."

"That is a false promise, and you know it. Don't deny you've been warned off talking with me."

Ammon dropped his hand and rubbed the back of his neck. "I won't deny it. Regardless of what my father has said, I will go against his wishes if your safety is involved."

"My safety. Surely, they wouldn't hurt me."

"Perhaps not, but they could still say things that you shouldn't hear. There are only hired hands working there now, and most of them are from other places." Since almost everyone was from someplace else, I assumed he meant they were not church-going men.

The earnest look on his face almost convinced me. "But I needed some rocks."

"I'll get you whatever rocks you need. Please don't go up alone."

"Please" was the only word I would have listened to. It wasn't often a woman heard that word when a man was trying to tell her what to do. Ammon wasn't trying to control me. "I can't be seen with you either."

"I know."

We stared at each other for a long moment. Something I couldn't identify passed between us. Ammon drew a breath. "The oxen are slow. Hurry ahead and find the footpath. I have to go around the far way over the canal bridge and double back."

I heeded his words. Not that he gave me much choice in the matter. When I reached the footpath, I turned back and waved. Ammon tipped his hat at me.

After dinner, Em sent me to the cellar around back of the cabin to bring up some potatoes for Sunday dinner she had forgotten to get earlier. I took a lantern with me.

A man stepped out of the shadow near the stable. I nearly shrieked before recognizing Ammon. "What are you doing here? You gave me a fright!"

"I wanted to be sure you arrived back safely." He came almost to the edge of the circle of lantern light.

My heart kept racing but to a slightly different beat—one that excited me more than scared me. "As you see, the only scare I've had is you. Were you waiting for me? How did you know I'd come out?"

"I was going to come to the house after I checked on things for Grandma. We'll get snow tonight or early tomorrow."

"Oh." I couldn't think of anything to say, and as much as I wanted to talk to him, I shouldn't. "I need to get potatoes."

"I'll hold the lantern."

We returned to the cabin together. Grandma Em laid out two slices of her oat cake. "I thought I heard you back there. Sit and have a bite before you go back down to your place. Will it be warm enough there, Ammon?"

"My stove came in. I set it up in the cellar. It's like living in one of the dugouts I've read about. Only my walls are square, and the floor and walls are lined with smooth slabs of quarry rock. I've spread canvas over the floor above my head to protect it from the snow and rain, so I don't have a leaky roof. The wall is up to five feet. I'll be snug this winter. And my barn is complete."

"I guess sleeping in a cave is better than sleeping with that old ox." Grandma Em sat in the rocking chair to eat her own cake.

Ammon laughed. I enjoyed their conversation. Again, he didn't speak directly to me, neither did I to him. I wanted to ask him questions about his house, but that could be seen as being more interested in him than I should be.

I waited until Ammon left to clean up. "Did you really need potatoes?"

"I can use them for tomorrow." Grandma Em evaded my question.

"You know I can't be seen with him, right? Someone spread a lie about us holding hands. My teaching contract forbids me from courting."

"I know all of that. I also know that teaching may not be the only thing that brought you to the valley." Grandma Em opened her Bible and began her nightly reading.

If she was insinuating God brought me to Cache Valley to marry, then someone forgot to notify Ammon's father, Ammon, and me.

§➤

As November grew colder, the children who stayed at school during the lunch hour started staying inside on days when the cold wind blew. Afternoons were often interrupted as the younger children fidgeted, bumping slates off of tables and each other. Even the older children struggled to sit still. I wished more than once a day for front-facing desks.

The Monday before Thanksgiving, we were reading the Presidential proclamation on Thanksgiving from the newspaper.

Just as Beth finished reading the second paragraph, the bench on the boys' side of the room tipped over, sending all seven boys sprawling onto the floor. The youngest, David Baker, hit his head on the bench I used for lessons in front of my desk. Lucy pointed to the blood on the floor and fainted, falling off her bench. Beth had caught her. Mary had the presence of mind to dip her handkerchief in the water pail and pressed it to David's head. Everyone yelled and talked at once.

I rang my hand bell to no avail. Sticking my little fingers between my lips, I did something I hoped never to do as a teacher—I whistled my high shrill whistle.

Everyone stopped.

"Boys, put your bench to rights and sit down. Mary, don't move David. Beth, help Lucy to the chair at my desk, and Lucy, look out the window." I pulled the napkin out of my lunch bucket and shook off the crumbs.

I knelt by David. "Mary, press this to his head on top of your handkerchief."

David blinked up at me. Conscious was good. There was more blood than I expected.

"Nathan, run for the doctor." I had no idea who or where the closest one was. Only after he left did I remember that the nearest doctor may be in Logan.

"Lucy, can you read the next chapter in *Little Women*?" If she was reading, she couldn't look at the blood.

"Yes, Miss Hardy." Lucy's soft voice wobbled.

The door opened with a bang, letting in a gust of wind. Nathan entered with Ammon.

"I'll take him to Grandma's. Send for his mother." Ammon scooped David up and ran out the door.

I looked around the room. David's sister, Anna, was ten, and they lived a mile from the school. Tears dripped down her face. I doubted she'd make it past Skidmores before she sat down and cried at the side of the road.

Mary's voice answered my dilemma. "I'll g-go, M-miss H-hardy. I can run f-f-fast."

I wouldn't have to worry about Mary getting lost, and I didn't think the stutter was an impediment to getting help. "Go, Mary."

She rushed to put on her coat, her shoulders straight and her eyes bright.

I used the cloth I kept to wipe off my blackboard to clean the blood off the floor as Lucy continued to read. The children cast worried glances out the window.

Lucy finished the chapter, and I took the book from her. "Get out your slates, please. We are going to practice our correspondence skills. I would like you to write a letter. You have two choices: a letter of comfort to David or a letter to me with an idea to prevent an accident like this from happening again. Once you have the letter the way you like it and I have approved it, you may put it to paper. I want to see your best penmanship. There are examples of good letters in the back of your readers." Everyone but Anna started writing. I called her up to my desk. "Would you like to draw your brother a picture?"

At her nod, I pulled out two pieces of paper and a set of colored drawing pencils.

Mary returned a half hour before school let out. She reported that David was doing well, and his mother was with them. Anna was to go to Grandma Woods's after school, and Mr. Ammon would drive them all home. The class let out a collective sigh of relief and finished their writing projects. No one chose to write me a letter with ideas to keep from having another accident.

I rang the bell dismissing the children. Mary walked Anna up the hill to Grandma Em's. I hoped Ammon would give the girl a ride home as well. Owen, the oldest boy, brought two loads of firewood into the school to be ready for the next day. He stood in front of my desk, shifting his weight from one foot to another.

"Miss Hardy?"

"Yes, Owen?"

"It was my fault. I was rocking on the bench and I pushed too hard. I'm sorry."

I doubted he had been the only one, but I wasn't sure if I should tell him. "I haven't seen Mr. Ammon's wagon go by. I'm sure you could run up and apologize to David."

"I'm aiming to do that. I just wanted to tell you I have a solution. Cut the bench in half. Then you won't have the little boys on the same bench as the big ones."

"That's a good idea, but I don't have a saw."

"I do. Me and my Pa could come fix it tonight."

"I like your solution. If I am not here, you can come get the key."

Owen grinned and rushed from the room.

I checked my watch. How long I would have to wait to hear from Mr. Skidmore? Ammon's wagon rumbled past. Mrs. Baker sat in front with Ammon. Mary, David, and his sister huddled in the back under one of Em's quilts. David's head was covered with a cap so I couldn't see his head. No one looked overly worried, and I hoped he'd be back in a day or two. I waited another fifteen minutes before closing the school. Maybe Mr. Skidmore wouldn't visit today.

Five

Moroni and Cornelia extended their invitation to Thanksgiving dinner to include me at her home in Hyde Park. Having no other place to go and not wanting Grandma Em to worry about me, I accepted, determined to stay out of every one's way—especially Ammon's. We arrived early in the morning with the pies Grandma Em had made the day before. The women kept busy in the kitchen. I did whatever I could do to help and stay out of the way, keenly aware that the day was for families. Moroni's house was a new home with room in the gabled attic. I'd grown so used to Grandma Em's cabin, that the house seemed enormous to me, although in reality it was smaller than my father's home in Salt Lake.

The tables were set with an array of dishes including both a duck and a large rooster, potatoes, bread and white rolls, baked squash, stewed tomatoes, and every other garden vegetable, mince and apple pies, and Grandma Em's pumpkin custard. The children had everyday dishes while the tables for the adults had hand-painted china. When we finally gathered for the meal, I found myself opposite Ammon and a young lady, Jannette, who had come from Logan with his brother Joseph and his wife. She wasn't a teacher. After every few bites, she smiled shyly at Ammon.

I tried not to look at either of them. It wasn't fair that I wasn't free to converse with him for fear of my job. My conversation was largely occupied by Cornelia and the many blessings the family had experienced during the year.

After dinner, I washed dishes along with the other women. Jannette didn't join us. While wiping down the table in the dining room, I heard laughter from the front porch. She sat on the swing with Ammon. Clearly someone's matchmaking efforts were bearing fruit. I hurried back into the kitchen and avoided Ammon until it was time to return home.

Grandma Em rode in the front seat, so I further managed to avoid conversation with him on the way home. I spent the entire time reminding myself that I was only here to teach. It was better that he had a girl, anyway.

At the cabin, I handed out the empty tins and baskets to Ammon and Grandma Em. I had worn one of my fashionable dresses to the dinner and had to wait for assistance to climb out of the back of the wagon. I would have preferred to jump down myself, but I knew I'd either rip the skirt or twist an ankle. Ammon opened the tailgate of the wagon. I set my hands on his shoulders as he lifted me down, just as I had that morning and every week at church. I ignored the warmth from his hands on my waist I dropped my hands the moment my feet touched the ground.

Ammon dropped his hands but didn't step back. "You were silent at dinner today."

"It was lovely to hear all the ways your family has been blessed this year." I tried to step around him.

"Jerusha, you can still talk to me. That isn't forbidden in your contract."

I looked up. He was standing so close that I had to lift my chin. "I don't want to cause any more problems between you and your family."

Ammon stepped back. I couldn't read the look on his face. I hurried into the cabin and up to my loft to remove my coat. Ammon didn't follow me into the house. Grandma Em informed me that she needed to rest and disappeared behind her curtain.

I started a new letter to my mother. How many of my siblings had been home today? What would they have been thankful for? What was I thankful for?

Mr. Skidmore hadn't reprimanded me for the accident at the school. By the time he came Tuesday afternoon, Owen and his father had already turned the long bench into two short ones and done the same for the girls' bench. This required the building of a new set of legs for the ends of two of the benches. Owen's father provided the lumber. David returned to class with a bandage around his head since Em had sewn his head with just two stitches of silk thread she kept expressly for the purpose. The bandage was to keep the area clean. I resorted to having him keep his knit cap on so he wouldn't be tempted to show the other children the stitches over and over again.

Overall, I was thankful for the opportunity to experience a place other than Salt Lake City. I was especially grateful that I could stay with Grandma Em. She was a never-ending well of information and stories.

I wrote to my mother all of these things. I asked about my siblings and concluded my letter with the story of the potbelly stove map. Most of it had since rubbed off the stove, which was just as well—I didn't want little fingers getting burned.

Grandma Em still slept as the sun started to set. I changed into a more functional skirt and checked on the chickens and the goat. I filled the woodbox and moved another two armfuls of wood to the corner of the porch. My moving around must have woken Grandma Em as she was awake when I returned to the cabin.

"Thank you for seeing to things for me. I must be getting old. I didn't used to need naps during the day."

"There is nothing like a well-earned nap."

Em laughed. "What did you think of Jannette?"

"She seemed nice enough." I set water on to boil. I wasn't hungry, however some apple peel tea would help warm me up.

"I was disappointed that she didn't come help us in the kitchen. I would have liked to get to know her better." Em didn't elaborate, and it wasn't my place to ask.

"The meal was lovely. The perfect amount of food."

"Cornelia always had a knack of planning those things. Like those women in England in the books you like so much."

"If we had grand balls, I'm sure she'd excel."

"She does plan many of the ones for her ward."

I'd never thought about it before, but many of our church functions were much like the ball at Netherfield, where eligible young ladies were foisted upon unsuspecting bachelors before they became a burden upon society. The men, not the women. "Hyde Park ward is very fortunate then."

Em looked as if she would say something, then shook her head. I poured our tea.

"I've experienced many Thanksgiving days in my life. Some, like this one, at the behest of the president, others because we were so thankful to have anything. I was there when we fought off the crickets in 1848 and the seagulls came. I've had so many things to be thankful for. I wonder if your generation even understands what it was like to cross the plains on foot. Now the railroad takes so few days. I heard a woman complain not too long ago about the rough ride she experienced on the train coming from Chicago because they could only afford third class and the benches were uncomfortable. Her journey was accomplished in a hundred days less than mine, and she wasn't in the family way."

"I try to be thankful." I said by way of defense. I'd only been nine when the railroad came to Utah and admittedly hadn't known much want.

Em waved a dismissive hand at me. "You don't complain, and you help. The biggest part of gratitude is accepting what you have. Would I like a big house like the one I had in Nauvoo? Not now.

I'd only have to clean it. This place is perfect for my needs, and you are the best of boarders."

Em continued to reminisce about being asked to come to the valley with her daughter and son-in-law, outliving all of her children and husband, and the years of scarcity. "I'm afraid I've reached that age where I look back and so much has changed. My grandfather used to tell me stories about fighting during the Revolution and meeting General Washington. He once told me that because he shook my hand that I could always say I shook the hand of a man who shook the hand of the first president of the United States. Made me proud to stand four years ago during the centennial celebration to think I had a link like that."

"Would you like to come talk to my class? Most of them don't have grandparents in the valley, if they have them at all."

"I don't know what I'd say," protested Em.

"Things like what you've been telling me. I'll loan you one of my history books. There is so much that you can say you were alive for."

"I'll think on it."

I added another log to the stove, and we turned down the light. By the time I was eighty, what would I have experienced?

The second week of December, we received our first notable snowfall in the valley. I'd woken up several mornings to snow on the surrounding mountains or a dusting on the ground that disappeared by noon.

Large, puffy flakes fell and snatched every student's attention to the window. At lunchtime, the students who stayed at school ate quickly and ran out to play. No one complained that it was too cold to go play. I kept watch through the window. A wagon pulled up and Mary's father climbed down. She followed him into the school building.

Mr. Flick didn't bother taking off his hat. "I'm here to take home the children who live out my way."

The look on his face kept me from protesting that school wasn't over and it was only a few inches of snow. "Mary, will you ring the outside bell?"

Over half of the remaining children left with him. He promised to stop by the Skidmores and tell them not to come back to school. A half hour later, another father came and took the rest of the children home.

I cleaned the room. The fire in the potbelly stove was slow to burn down. I poked at it and considered adding a few snowballs. Finally, it reached the point I felt I could safely leave the building. No one wanted to be known as the teacher who burned down the school. When it was finally out, I bundled up and extinguished the lantern. The wind whipped around me as I struggled to pull the door closed and lock it. Rounding the schoolhouse, I was shocked to see that I couldn't see anything but a world of white. A shadow where the tall pine stood near the outhouse was the only landmark. I'd read stories of people lost in blizzards. A few years ago, a teacher somewhere in the East lost his life trying to return home after delivering all of his students safely to their homes. If this storm was anything like the ones in Salt Lake, in an hour or so, I'd be unable to make my way safely home. Then it would be dark.

I took a few steps in the direction of the outhouse. The wind pushed against me. Snow blew in my face. The only thing I could see was the wall of the school behind me.

I returned to the schoolroom.

The room was still warm. I took note of the time on my watch. 2:35. In an hour, if I didn't think I could return to Em's safely, I'd start the fire again. I lit the lantern and placed it near the window and prayed Grandma Em would know I had enough sense to stay put. I pulled out the copy of Jules Verne's *Around the World in Eighty Days*. I'd never read it and wanted to make sure it wouldn't be too scary for the younger children. I was crossing the continent by rail with Mr. Fogg when the door banged open. Snowflakes entered with Ammon.

"Grandma has been waiting for you for over an hour."

"Has it stopped blowing?" A glance out of the window answered my own question. All I could see was the tree across the street.

"Only just. Let's get you home. I need to return to my place before the wind or the storm pick back up again."

Ammon helped me with my coat and checked the stove while I put on my scarf. I extinguished the lantern, plunging the school-room into deep shadow. After I locked the door, Ammon took my hand and dragged me along behind him. I reasoned that any gentleman would protect a lady in such a predicament, yet I knew I should not hold his hand. I let go of Ammon's hand and lifted my skirt. I followed this footsteps in the snow which was eight inches or more deep. Matching my strides to his wasn't easy but better than the snow slipping inside my boots. He stopped and waved me to hurry.

I stomped as much snow off of my feet as I could at Grandma Em's porch. The snow clung to the hem of my skirt.

Em looked up from the pot she stirred over the stove. "I told you she was smart enough to stay at the school. Jerusha, you best go change out of those wet clothes. Ammon, stand over here—" She pointed to a spot under the loft. "—and warm for a moment."

"Warming up will make it that much harder to go back out. I'd best leave now and go home. My horse is saddled and wait-ing for me."

I paused on the bottom stair. "Thank you for retrieving me."

Ammon nodded and was out the door before the melting snow puddled around his feet.

"Go on, get in dry clothes, now. You don't need to catch cold over this."

I was halfway up the stairs when Em added, "Then you can come mop the floor. I just finished when it started to snow."

The week before Christmas came before I was ready for it. Between term grades, social functions, and finding gifts, I was busy from dawn to dusk.

The schoolhouse was far too small to hold the families of the students, so I promised the children we would put on a play and recitation around the first of May when school ended and we could gather out of doors. Several children brought me small gifts they'd made: an embroidered handkerchief, a lopsided scarf, a cloth for the blackboard. My favorite was a button necklace from the Baker children. Anna informed me she'd collected a button from every student for it.

I made sure the fire was completely dowsed before locking up the school for a week. The only book I took home was the Jules Verne. I thought I might need to skip over some details of the opium den and Aouda's rescue from being burned alive, but I wanted a second opinion and planned to read it to Grandma Em.

A large package arrived from Salt Lake for me. Em put it under her bed so I wouldn't be tempted to open it before Christmas morning. I also received an invitation to a social for teachers from all over the valley, to be held on the Tuesday after Christmas and hosted by Brigham Young College. It would be the first time that I would meet any teachers in the area. Finally, a social event where I wouldn't be expected to stand behind a refreshment table the entire event.

Finding a gift for Grandma Em proved difficult. Inspiration hit while I wandered through the bookstore in Logan. I purchased a blank journal. After school, I stayed late, writing stories she shared with me over the months. The book wasn't so much for her as for her grandchildren to pass on the stories to their children. Grandma Em avoided writing. I assumed it hurt her hands, which were gnarled with age. Often, she'd pass me the pencil and paper and have me add to her grocery list.

Ammon was more difficult. It was inappropriate to give him anything personal or anything at all. Yet I wanted to thank him for the help rendered me during the term. A gift was a way I could express something of the friendship we were denied. I decided on a pair of leather work gloves. Useful and not flirtatious at all.

Christmas fell on a Thursday. Joseph Junior and his wife Elmira invited Grandma Em to his house in Logan for Christmas Day along with Ammon. My invitation came as an afterthought following Em's prodding. As none of my students' families invited me for the day, I accepted the invitation. As I had on Thanksgiving, I endeavored to be quiet and helpful for the Christmas dinner. I shooed Grandma Em out of the kitchen more than once so she could sit with her grandchildren and great-grandchildren.

To my chagrin, Jannette attended as well. Once again, she didn't help in the kitchen beyond carrying in a few dirty plates. I told Elmira I could finish the cleaning while she sat with the family. I caught glimpses of the fun as I cleaned. Ammon sat on the settee next to Jannette, laughing over the pictures in the stereoscope. I wished I could sit with them—or at least Ammon. I had no desire to further my acquaintance with Jannette. I longed to have an entire conversation with him, not just the snippets we shared at Grandma Em's.

I'd set the first of the large pans soaking when a hush fell on the parlor and I heard the first verses of Luke. Drying my hands on my apron, I walked to the doorway and listened. I stayed in the shadows, because this wasn't my family, house, or tradition. When the reading concluded, the family started singing.

A sudden longing for my own family filled me. My father's rich baritone, mother's alto, and my sister's soprano. We were a nice choir, and not to think rudely of my hosts, but they were slightly off-key. I returned to the dishes and hummed along with the songs they sang. I'd just finished the last pan when Ammon entered the kitchen. "Why didn't you join us?"

I folded the towel and laid it next to the dry sink. "I needed to do this more."

"Night is falling, and Grandma is ready to go home."

I nodded and followed him out of the room. Grandma Em collected hugs and kisses from each of the children.

After putting on my coat, I returned to the kitchen to gather the warmed quilts from behind the stove. Elmira wrapped three potatoes in flannel and put them in a basket for us. She followed me to the front door.

Jannette stood close to Ammon, her back to me. "I was so sad to learn that mistletoe doesn't grow in Utah. You've missed out on that tradition."

He cleared his throat and stepped back. His sister-in-law handed him the basket. "Will you take these out for me?"

Jannette turned at the sound of Elmira's voice and leveled a glare at me. Did she realize that I heard her all but beg for a kiss? I nodded politely as I passed.

Joseph Junior helped Grandma Em with her coat. Ammon came back in and took the blankets from me.

He nodded to his brother. "Thank you for the use of your buggy. I'll return it Monday."

Relief filled me. Unlike Ammon's open buckboard, the buggy provided some shelter from the elements. Ammon helped Grandma Em into the seat, then me. Grandma sat in the middle, where she would be the warmest. Other than her naps, which she'd taken daily since Thanksgiving, there was nothing besides her age that gave me alarm for her. I wondered if Ammon knew she was slowing down. But I couldn't ask, not in front of Grandma Em.

Six

THE WARD PARTY WAS HELD the following night. I was asked to serve at the punch bowl and refreshment table at the dance held by the church. As a female teacher, I was expected to work the refreshment tables at all social functions. Then no one needed to feel awkward since I wouldn't have an escort and shouldn't dance much. The request might have been less condescending if it hadn't come from Mrs. Skidmore.

Grandma Em and I came with the Skidmores rather than Ammon. I didn't ask why. Grandma Em brought a large basket of gingerbread rounds, which I took to the refreshment tables. Mrs. Baker directed me in my duties: Keep the punch bowl filled. There was more punch in pitchers in the other room. Beware of anyone attempting to add anything to the punch.

Apparently, there had been a problem last spring when someone from the out-of-town teamsters attended and they'd added a bottle of gin.

The teenage boys needed to be watched, she continued to guide me, so as to not eat all the goodies. If I needed to leave the table for any reason, I needed to have her or one of the other ladies in charge take my place.

"But since you won't be dancing, you should have no reason to leave." At least five different people, including Mr. Skidmore, uttered a version of that sentence.

Across the room, fiddlers tuned their instruments. Families split apart as children found friends, fathers discussed the next year's crops, and mothers talked about anything. A few couples came in. I recognized most of them from church.

I was utterly unprepared for Jannette to enter on Ammon's arm. Before, I assumed her presence was a manipulation of his family, but they hadn't brought her. He had. I handed out a cup of punch to a young mother and tried not to follow Ammon's progress across the floor. It was for the best. Mrs. Skidmore couldn't start any more rumors about my lack of decorum. Ammon would be doubly sure not to associate with me if he was courting. I had no hold on him nor right to hold him. Still, my heart ached.

An hour later, Ammon appeared on the other side of the serving table. "Two cups of punch please."

I handed them to him. "Enjoy."

He took one step away from the table and turned back. "Would you like to dance?"

"I can't." I smiled my best apologetic smile.

"You're sure? Jannette is sitting the next few out." He didn't call her Miss.

"I've been told not to leave the table. Enjoy the dance." I watched him walk away until someone else came for punch. He should have known better than to ask me to dance with his father and the entire ward there. I'd had a few polite offers from men that night. The only offer I'd been tempted to take was little David, but no one was near enough to take my place.

We closed the refreshment table before the dance ended. I found myself in a corner washing dozens of cups and setting them out for the women to collect and take home. Many of them had been marked with a piece of thread around the handle so I grouped them by sets. Soon families with young children left, and the band announced their final song. I gathered my coat and Grandma Em's and went in search of her.

She sat in a chair next to another woman near her age. "Did you dance?"

"No, I kept busy, though, and was able to greet almost everyone here."

Mr. and Mrs. Skidmore joined us. Ammon and Jannette danced by me. I turned my head away and focused on helping Grandma Em into her coat.

I don't know why I couldn't force my heart not to pay attention to Ammon.

I arrived before noon at the gymnasium for the teacher social, having gotten a ride with Mr. Skidmore, who needed to go to the Z.C.M.I. Finally, I would get to meet Miss Ida Cook, the principal of Brigham Young College. I had so many questions for her, mostly about Mary. I'd tucked a page from Mary's last arithmetic test and a report she'd written on the Constitution into my handbag. The room was more than half full of teachers who also arrived early. I recognized two others from my class at the University of Deseret and went to talk with them.

Miss Adamson was several inches taller than me and wore her glasses perched on the end of her nose. "Jerusha! I didn't know you were teaching in the valley."

"It was a last-minute post. I am at the Green Canyon school. Where are you posted?" I asked.

"Mendon. Miss Edwards teaches with me. We have so many students that sometimes Mr. Martin has taken the older students over to the jail for class."

"Assuming it is empty of course." Miss Edwards giggled, more for Mr. Martin's benefit than mine. "How many students do you have?"

"I started with fifteen but added three more. The youngest children sit in front of my desk now. I don't think we could fit any more children in, although I am aware that many children still don't have a place to go to school."

The woman nodded their agreement. A thin man with a receding hairline joined us. Miss Adamson introduced him as Mr. Shaw.

"Pleasure to meet you, Miss Hardy." He turned to the other teachers. "I came over to ask if you would each save a dance for me. I've been promised we will have dancing after the luncheon." Both women agreed, and he turned to me. "I suppose you would also be agreeable to me as partner. The third dance will be yours."

Before I could answer, he walked off.

Neither Miss Adamson nor Miss Edwards wore shocked expressions. We decided that we should mingle and started a circuit around the room. There were more women than men. A few of the men had wives at their side. If there was to be a dance, the numbers were terribly skewed. Miss Edwards met with another friend, and I left her and Miss Adamson and continued around on my own. A woman in a dark dress several inches taller than me but at least a decade older stood alone.

"Hello, I'm Jerusha Hardy, Green Canyon School."

"Welcome to our school. I'm Miss Cook."

"I've wanted to meet you for the longest time." I was unsure if I should stick my hand out or give her a hug.

Her laugh was rich and deep. "I don't usually get such an enthusiastic response from young teachers. They seem to think I either want to recruit them to the college or critique their work."

"I need advice. I have a very bright student who has been overlooked for years because of a stutter. Most of her teachers have given her very poor marks because she can't stand in front of a class and recite her lessons." I pulled out Mary's papers. "Would you mind looking at these and get back to me?"

"I have a few moments now." Miss Cook led me over to a set of chairs in a corner, reading the papers as she walked. She folded the papers and handed them back to me. "She does seem very bright. Have you any plans for her?"

"I have heard that the college has a bookkeeping course. I wondered if she might be a candidate. Even if she could get a teaching certificate, no one would hire her. My other thought is midwifery or perhaps nursing. We had an incident with an injured child, and she seemed to know what to do with him. However, I don't believe a college in the East would keep her because of the stutter."

Miss Cook pinched her lips. "Unfortunately, you are probably correct. I will talk to the teacher over the bookkeeping. How old is she?"

"Almost sixteen."

"Then she could enter next fall. May I keep those papers after all?"

I handed them back. "Thank you."

"It was nice to meet you, Miss Hardy."

We parted, and I continued to mingle. We did have dancing, and my only dance was with Mr. Shaw, who stepped on my toes. The social ended at three-thirty. Mr. Skidmore wasn't there. I waited another half hour as all the teachers departed. Many of them had brought borrowed horses or rigs.

I had few choices. In the dark and the cold, walking five miles was daunting. I walked the few blocks to Joseph Junior's home in hopes of securing a ride. Even if they had a sidesaddle, I couldn't borrow a horse as my skills were so poor.

Elmira answered the door, her eyes wide. "Miss Hardy, wherever did you come from?"

I explained my plight.

"I think I might have a solution. Come into the kitchen and warm up."

I followed her, wanting nothing more than to warm my fingers and toes.

I stood near the stove as Elmira set meat pies on a platter on the table. "Some of Joseph's employees had an outing today—ice skating. I promised them something warm when they return."

"May I help?"

"No, I have it well in hand." She took the platter into the dining room. Minutes later, the front door opened and laughter filled the house. As curious as I was, I didn't investigate. The voices filtered through the house in my mind as I pictured three or four women and several men. I picked out Jannette's high-pitched squeal. I was glad to be cloistered in the kitchen until I heard Ammon's voice.

Was that Elmira's plan: to send me home with him after he spent the afternoon courting Jannette? This would never do. I might be a lowly teacher, but I had some pride. The clock on the wall told me it was still before five. Perhaps Mr. Skidmore had gotten the times confused. I should go back to the gymnasium. Hastily, I wrapped my scarf around my face, put my gloves back on, and slipped out of the back door without a sound.

No one waited at the gymnasium. I went to the Z.C.M.I., hoping that someone from my area would have had a late errand. The door was locked. If I walked swiftly, I could keep warm, and I knew that during the summer I could walk a mile in a quarter hour. Clouds obscured the moon. Nevertheless, I should be able to find my way and be at Grandma Em's before seven. I was six blocks north when I heard my name called.

Ammon sat astride his horse. "Why didn't you stay at Joe's?"

"I cannot accept a ride from you."

"You can when it is my father's fault you're stranded."

"I can't when you're courting."

He dismounted. "And I can't let you walk home."

"Since I don't ride and you can't walk home either, we are at an impasse."

"You don't ride?"

"I've always been able to walk where I needed to." I wasn't being exactly truthful. Father would drive us or hire a driver. "It is less than five miles. I can walk it."

Ammon stepped closer. "On a warm spring day, but not now."

"I don't see that I have a choice." I ignored a snowflake that fell on Ammon's shoulder and the next one that passed between us.

Ammon cast a glance heavenward, whether in prayer or to find the source of the flakes, I wasn't sure. "We need to hurry."

"And you are delaying me." I turned to continue my walk.

Ammon grabbed my elbow. "Get on my horse."

I wasn't intimidated by the large animal. I wasn't afraid of horses, per se, but more of falling off of them. Plus, there was no way I could climb onto the horse without hoisting my skirts up to my knees. Not to mention my bustle. "I can't."

With one quick move, Ammon clasped me about my waist and settled me sideways on the saddle. Before I could protest, he swung up behind me and pulled me to him.

I gripped the pommel with one hand and my hat with the other. "Ammon! We can't ride this way."

The horse responded to his command, proving my words were not about a physical impossibility.

"My horse and I disagree."

"It isn't proper. What will your father say?" Or rather, his stepmother. "I need my job."

"He'll apologize for leaving you in town."

I tried to lean away from Ammon's chest. He responded by pulling me closer. "Stop wiggling. You'll upset the horse."

"Your stepmother will—" The wind picked up, blowing a strand of hair into my face and pulling at my hat. The hat offered little protection as it wasn't meant to be worn in a snowstorm.

"My stepmother won't know. She won't see us." Ammon turned east at the next street.

Others might see us. Although it would be hard to tell who we were in the falling snow. I wanted to point out that Jannette wouldn't be pleased either. With trying to not lean on Ammon, hold on to the pommel, and keep my hat on my head, I couldn't keep the hair out of my mouth long enough to speak.

"Lean against me. It will be easier for all of us." Ammon pulled me back again.

Easier for the horse and him, but not for me. Even if it was warmer. Cocooned in his embrace, it was impossible not to think of Ammon and how I wish he could hold me forever. Even more impossible not to think of Jannette and the scandal I would cause. If any member of the school board saw us now, I would lose my job for certain. If I was already to lose it, I may as well save my fingers from frostbite. I moved my frozen hand from the pommel to the front of his coat.

Ammon adjusted his grip on me. I wished for my wool-lined bonnet; it would have been a much better choice. The feathers of this hat were no doubt ruined, if they were still there at all. The wind continued to tug on the hat strongly enough that the hatpin pulled my hair. Ammon turned another corner, and my hat blew in the direction of his face.

"I need to take off my hat! Can you slow for a moment?"

There was no response. I located my hatpin, and with frozen fingers, managed to pull it out. With the next gust, my hat took a journey, presumably south. I tucked my hatpin into the front of my coat, careful not to catch myself on its six-inch spike. No longer needing my hand to hold onto the hat, I wrapped my arm around Ammon and leaned further into his chest and out of the cold.

Soon he slowed his horse. I lifted my head and saw the outline of Grandma Em's cabin. He stopped in front of the door and handed me down without dismounting.

"I'll tell my father you are safely home." Ammon turned his horse, and they trotted away.

Grandma Em had bolted the door against the wind. I knocked.

"Hurry in. The wind is getting worse." Grandma Em closed and bolted the door behind me. "I expected you home over an hour ago."

"There was some confusion about my ride back from town." I struggled out of my coat, finally realizing that my hat pin held it tight to my dress. My frozen fingers struggled to remove it.

"How did you get home?"

"Ammon. Please excuse me while I change out of this dress."

I escaped upstairs. I'd come to know Grandma Em well enough that I was afraid she might see everything I didn't want to say. It didn't matter anyway. Ammon had Jannette. There would be no chance that in four months when I was free to court, he would still be available. How could I feel such loss for something I never had?

Seven

JANUARY WAS BITTERLY COLD. THE snow never seemed to melt before the next round hit. The classroom lantern remained on most days. During the lunch hour, I'd adopted a routine of calisthenics for the children. The boys turned it into a competition, as they are wont to do. They kept a tally of who did the most push-ups. The classroom wasn't large enough for everyone to do the exercises at once. The girls only participated in the marching in place and stretches as some movements in dresses in an enclosed space were too difficult to do. Between the exercise and smaller benches, we had no more accidents

It was still a struggle to keep their attention as the days dragged on. Mid-month, three students missed class. The next day two more were absent. The doctor stopped by and told me that they had several cases of measles and asked me to close down the school for a week, possibly two. I wrote notes to send home to each family and posted a sign on the door. I sent the children's readers and arithmetic books with them and asked them to read a section a day and also do a page of math as long as they were well.

Measles was but a faint memory in my mind, having only been three when I stared the sickbed with my siblings. Mary and a few of the older students said they'd already had measles but didn't argue with the doctor about closing the school. With a third of my students out, I wasn't upset either, as I wouldn't want to teach any of the bigger classroom lessons more than once.

The children helped me clean the classroom and bring in wood for when school did start again. I allowed them to leave a half hour early as they lost their concentration, and I had no motivation to teach. I locked up the building and trudged through the slushy snow to Em's.

She looked up from her knitting. "Did the doctor close the school?"

"Yes. A third of my students are already sick."

"Best to get measles over while they are young."

"I have time to help you with that quilt now."

Em laughed. "That you do."

A week turned into two. I received the geology book I had been waiting for and spent several hours reading and planning. As soon as the ground dried enough to walk the roads without collecting inches of mud, I'd take the children rock hunting. Em advised me to wait until the end of February.

I also received a letter from Miss Cook with an invitation for Mary to apply to the college. I wanted to deliver the message in person, but they still had a quarantine sign on their door. Mary's oldest sister's family had moved in shortly before Christmas. I'd heard all four children had contracted the measles, including the baby.

Grandma Em and I sewed two quilt tops from the scraps she'd collected. Ammon came by each day to check on Em but never stayed long. We hadn't spoken more than five words since the night he'd dropped me off after the party. If the weather was fair, I'd take a walk when he came so he and Em could chat. I'd walk up the hill and watch for him to leave before I returned. When it was raining or snowing, Ammon rarely stayed.

I may have been more relieved than the children when I was able to reopen the schoolhouse doors—until I learned one of my children would not be returning.

David was now deaf. His younger brother, who I'd only seen at church, had died.

The entire class moaned at the news. We did another class on letter writing and each wrote a letter to David.

"David can't hear, but he can read. He can play and can still be your friend." I urged them to include him in their activities.

After school, I went and visited David. I took his slate and slate pencil to him.

"I can't go to school no more." He greeted me loudly.

I wrote on the slate.

You can still learn.

"How?"

You can read. Many great men didn't go to school and learned by reading.

"I don't know all the words."

Inspiration struck.

Not yet, but you will.

David looked at me, his brow furrowed.

Anna stood watching.

Each day after school I want you to read to Anna. If you don't know a word, she can write what it means.

"What if I can't say it right?"

I didn't have an answer.

Don't worry too much about that right now. If you do this every day until the end of school, I'll give you my copy of Around the World in Eighty Days.

I'd have to talk to his mother about the opium den chapter. I was planning on downplaying it at school. At least we had already read about the rescue in India, where I'd conveniently glossed over some paragraphs. Burning a widow alive was not a subject I'd wanted to discuss.

Read with Anna now. I need to talk with your mother.

Mrs. Baker was in the kitchen of their four-room house, finishing dinner. Her movements were slow and deliberate.

"My condolences. The children wrote these letters to your family today."

Mrs. Baker took the papers and set them on a shelf without opening them. "Thank you for coming to see David. He is so upset that he can't go to school."

"I wish I knew how to teach deaf students. I have encouraged David to read out loud to his sister each day. I told him I would bring him a copy of *Around the World in Eighty Days*. We've been reading it in class, but I have been making a few modifications because I feared the content wasn't appropriate for all of my students. His book won't have those modifications, and there is a scene in an opium den."

She wiped her hands on a dishtowel. "If it keeps him interested in reading, I don't care what the book says. I just wish…" She blinked back tears.

I couldn't imagine how difficult this was for her. I had only one idea to offer hope. "There is a school for the deaf in Ogden. David isn't the only child who can't hear."

"Ogden is too far away. He only turned eight before Christmas." Her wan smile did little to hide her emotions.

"Perhaps by next fall then. David is a smart boy. Encourage him to read and figure out math problems. If he wants to write to me, I'll write back."

"Can you come to visit once a week?"

"Gladly."

David gave me a hug before I left.

February thawed into March. I started teaching about rocks and where they came from in short lessons at the end of the school day. I was afraid none of us could visualize a volcano and how rock melted and flowed like a river until Owen reminded us of the blacksmith.

Finally, the weather warmed enough that we went exploring, searching for different rocks. We took our lunches along and made a picnic of the day. Each student found a favorite rock to bring back to the school. Several found more than one.

We returned to the school an hour before end of day as I'd planned. A buggy I didn't recognize stood in the schoolyard. Two men in suits leaned in the doorway. I recognized Mr. Skidmore first.

I looked around at my students. Being tired from our excursion, they were well-behaved, albeit talkative. Each child clamored to tell about the rocks they had seen and discussed why some rocks were smooth and others jagged.

As we neared the schoolyard, both men turned their attention to us.

Mr. Skidmore took several steps in my direction. "Miss Hardy, where have you been?"

I turned to the children and instructed them to go rinse off their rocks and their hands while I spoke with Mr. Skidmore and the other gentleman. "We had an outing today. We've been studying geology, and we went in search of rocks to see how many varieties we could find."

Mr. Skidmore crossed his arms. "Why wasn't I informed?"

I had informed him of my intentions several weeks ago. I'd sent home notes with each of the students yesterday declaring that today everyone would need to bring a lunch as we would eat in the canyon. Seeing that all three of his children, who normally returned home for lunch, brought sandwiches neatly wrapped in paper, I could only assume that someone was aware of the outing.

I'd also tacked a note on the door stating that we had ventured up Green Canyon. Mr. Skidmore didn't wait for my reply.

"Mr. Welsh is here to inspect your teaching. How can he do that if you are not here?"

"Had I been aware of the inspection, I would have postponed our scientific investigation for another day." I looked at both men.

Mr. Welsh seemed to hide a smile. "That would take the surprise out of 'surprise inspection.' Do you often take your students on explorations?"

"This is the first one since the new year. With the stone quarries in the canyon and so many buildings being built from the stone, I added a section on geology to our studies."

"Will you gather your students? I wish to question them," said Mr. Welsh.

The possibility that I would have an inspection had occurred to me more than once. On several occasions, I'd talked to the children about such inspections. The older ones had already endured them and understood the need to be polite and answer the questions asked. In my mind, I'd pictured us in the classroom sitting primly in our bench seats, each face clean and scrubbed. As it was, the children had worn clothing usually reserved for chores at home, several of the girls' dresses were inches too short and, like the boys' pants, they sported patches. Dirt smudges covered everything from faces to knees. My own hair was in a simple braid hidden by a straw hat that kept the sun off my face. I gathered the children and sorted them into two lines in front of the school.

"Who would like to show me their rock?" asked Mr. Welsh. He ignored the raised hands and chose Anna. "What rock do you have?"

Anna held out a deep red-hued rock from the second quarry. "It is a red limestone, sir."

"What type of rock is limestone?"

Without looking around, Anna answered. "Sedimentary. This

is a very hard variety. They used it to build the Logan Temple and the Tabernacle."

"Very good." He pointed to Owen. "If it takes 13,500 tons of stone to build a house and the price is twenty-eight cents per ton, how much will it cost to build the house?"

"The stone will cost three-thousand-seven hundred and eighty dollars. They would still need wood, and nails and cement, and many other things."

Mr. Welsh chuckled. He pointed to Mary. "How do you spell 'metamorphic rock'?"

Mary's eyes grew wide. We'd practiced this type of question in the classroom. I told her that, like the spelling bee, she would be allowed to write it out. Nathan handed her a slate and slate pencil. He'd slipped in and out of the building so fast even I hadn't seen him.

Mary took the slate and wrote metamorphic rock. She handed it to Mr. Welsh. "I s-t-tutter. M-miss H-ha-hardy l-l-ets me-e-e writ-t-te."

Mr. Welsh handed her back the slate and went on to quiz the children about history and other things. In the end, each child had answered at least one question. Owen recited the first six stanzas of Paul Revere's Ride by Henry Wadsworth Longfellow, ending at, "But lingers and gazes, till full on his sight a second lamp in the belfry burns!" He could have finished the entire thing, but Mr. Welsh stopped him.

"I believe it is time for school to be dismissed. Miss Hardy, dismiss your students, then we will talk." Mr. Welsh started toward the buggy with Mr. Skidmore half a step behind.

The students set their rocks under their benches so we could discuss them tomorrow. I whispered compliments to each child on their answers to Mr. Welsh's questions.

I hugged Mary. "You were very brave."

She smiled. "N-n-no re-re-eciting. I could have done it."

"Yes, I'm happy he didn't ask you to recite a poem too."

Mr. Welsh and Mr. Skidmore entered the classroom after the last child left. Mr. Skidmore took my chair behind the desk.

"I remarked to Mr. Skidmore earlier that this seemed an odd layout for a school room."

"It is, but we have made it work. I use this short bench when I am working with a particular grade so that the children face me instead of the walls."

He turned to Mr. Skidmore. "Are there any plans to upgrade the school?"

"We are in the planning stage of a larger building to the north of here. We have more children than this school can hold. Greenville is growing. We will use this school as is for another year."

"Greenville?"

"That is what we decided to call this town. We have yet to incorporate."

"I hope you consider keeping on Miss Hardy. She is a capable teacher."

My heart soared. Capable was not the greatest of compliments, but considering the disastrous start to the visit, I was happy not to be dismissed.

Mr. Skidmore swallowed. "I will pass that on to the others in the school board. As I told you, we are considering another candidate."

He spoke as if I wasn't in the room. Another teacher? Would they love my students? Visit David? Mary would be at Brigham Young College, so at least a harsh teacher couldn't bully her. I bit my cheek to force myself not to react, knowing both men would see any outer reaction as weakness.

Mr. Welsh spoke to me. "Refreshing classroom. I wish all the teachers in the valley had your imagination."

My brain scrambled to catch what he said.

We shook hands, and the men left me in my silent classroom, still trying to absorb what I'd heard. I refused to cry, not here, not now. Later that night in my bed I could give in to tears.

Eight

Spring buds filled the valley. After school, I loved to climb the ridge and look across to the Wellsville Mountains. The tall sagebrush bloomed silver, and the sunlight reflected golden off of the marshland in the center of the valley. Each day, farmers prepared more land for planting, patchworking the scene in rich browns.

Each day was a day closer to my last day in the valley. A day I dreaded.

Mr. Skidmore hadn't extended a new contract to me, as Mrs. Skidmore's youngest brother would take the post. Em informed me she would not be providing room and board for the new teacher. She took longer and longer naps each day, a fact I mentioned to Ammon a week ago Saturday when he stopped and found me hoeing the garden to prepare it for Grandma Em's seeds.

His only answer was a quiet, "I know," before going on with repairing the goat pen.

The children worked on their recitations for their parents for the last night of school. They'd even concocted their own play based on *Around the World in Eighty Days*. They filled the dialogue with tidbits they'd learned, adding a stop where the golden spike had been driven just twenty-two years earlier. Mr. Fogg and Passepartout then detoured to Cache Valley, where they saw our fine limestone buildings and delicious apples. Mary pointed out this would make eighty-two days, a problem solved by not stopping in Singapore.

I didn't linger in the schoolhouse after school since Em needed more help. As I had done for several days, I made as much noise as possible when entering the cabin and changing into a work dress. Only today, Em didn't wake and come out from behind her curtain, pretending that she had been doing something other than sleeping.

"Grandma Em?"

No answer came. I called again. The faintest of moans reached my ears. I pulled back the curtain. Grandma Em's face looked lopsided. She lifted one shaky hand and pointed. "Amm."

"You want Ammon?"

Something in her face relaxed, and I knew I was right. I rushed out the door and cut across fields to the bench, the fastest way to his orchard and home. I followed a deer trail up the steep hill. My foot caught on a rock, and I fell to my knees. The deer were much nimbler than I.

I reached the corner of the apple orchard and ran north to the home site, yelling Ammon's name. What if he wasn't here? What if he was working on the agricultural college building or at the barns? What if he was with Jannette? I should have gone to the Skidmores' and begged someone to ride for a doctor and send someone with a horse after Ammon. I hadn't been thinking clearly. Now the swiftest course led me through the budding trees.

My yell scared a bird from her nest. She screeched at me as I ran past. An article in the newspaper last year spoke of men who ran a five-minute mile. The burning in my lungs told me that I may have joined their ranks, although it seemed like I'd run for hours, and Ammon's homesite was less than a mile by road. I rounded the barn and into Ammons arms. The impact landed me on my backside.

I struggled to get my breath while Ammon helped me up and asked the expected questions.

Waving him off, I held my side. "Grandma Em. Hurry."

Ammon swung up bareback onto his horse and thrust out his hand to pull me up behind him.

"Go! Just Go!"

"Get on!" Ammon yelled back at me.

Even if I was used to riding a saddled horse, I couldn't. His horse was too tall.

I waved my arm in the direction of Em's "Go. I'll come as fast as I can."

Ammon leapt down and threw me onto the horse's back. I landed astride with my skirts up around my knees with the air forced out of my starving lungs.

The next moment he was in front of me on the horse. "Hold on!"

The horse took off at thundering gallop. I wrapped my arms around Ammon's middle and prayed I wouldn't fall. Moments later, he pulled the horse to a stop at the door to Em's. He dismounted and lifted me off. My feet barely touched the ground before he through the door.

The next hour was one of chaos. Ammon commanded me to stay with Grandma while he went in search of the doctor.

"No, let me, I'll send your father or Nathan."

I was out the door before he could stop me. Running down a flat road for a quarter mile was nothing after the run I made to Ammon's. I returned with Mrs. Skidmore in my wake, crying and saying how much they would miss Grandma. Considering I'd never witnessed her give Grandma Em more than a polite nod, I didn't believe her. When we were still a distance from the cabin, I turned on her.

"Emeline's cabin is small. Perhaps you should wait at your own home for news. You'd be much more comfortable."

"But I should be there."

"Why? Your tears won't help her. If you can be useful, stay. If not, I'll send word."

"Well." Her tears dried up as she spun on her heel and turned back to her house.

I knew enough about horses to know that Ammon's shouldn't just stand there after being ridden hard. Yet I was too afraid to move him, so I just went inside.

Ammon sat on one of the straight-backed chairs next to Grandma's bed.

I dipped a clean dishcloth into the bucket of water, wrung it out, and handed it to Ammon. It always felt good to have my face washed when I felt unwell. Ammon looked at the cloth, then at me. I motioned wiping her forehead. Awkwardly, he followed my instructions. Grandma Em still wore her sturdy boots. I moved to the end of the bed and unlaced them.

"Should I do something for your horse? A bucket of water?"

Ammon's eyes met mine, questioning, as if he couldn't process the question. "I'll take care of him when the doctor comes."

Grandma Em made small noises and patted Ammon with her right hand. Ammon looked confused.

I listened carefully. Months of listening to Mary had given me a keen ear. "I think she wants you to read to her." I handed him Em's Bible and opened it to her favorite passage.

Ammon began reading the Beatitudes, and Em relaxed once again. Hearing the doctor's buggy in the yard, I rushed to open the door for him. The doctor asked me to stay while he examined Em. I helped change her clothes and get her into one of her soft nightgowns. The doctor spoke with Ammon outside of the door. I didn't need to hear to know the truth.

Not long after, Moroni and Joseph Junior arrived. Mrs. Skidmore's wagging tongue had found something useful to do. The doctor left. There was little anyone could do but watch and wait.

I did my best to stay out of the way. At dusk, Ammon's brothers returned to their homes.

Ammon resumed his seat next to Grandma Em. "Has she had anything to drink?"

"A bit of water, but it all dribbled out."

"Would you like me to leave so you can stay here tonight?"

"You need not leave… Oh, your job."

"I wasn't thinking of my job. Only that it might make you feel uncomfortable or make Jannette upset if I was to remain here with you."

"Why would Jannette care?"

"I thought you were courting."

Ammon's lips pinched together. "No, I am not courting her."

"But the dance, ice skating…" I clamped my hand over my mouth. Now was not the time to ask questions about her. Grandma Em was dying. I turned away.

Ammon's soft voice filled the room. "I took her to the dance at my brother's request, since I didn't have any other prospect I wanted to take. The ice skating was also at his behest. I believe Elmira thought she was playing matchmaker."

"But you talked for so long at Thanksgiving dinner and again at Christmas."

"Correction—she talked, I was cornered. I nearly came and dragged you out of the kitchen at Christmas. The skating party was the final straw. She pretended not to know now to skate and tripped me twice only to land with her mouth on mine. That is why I was so angry that night."

"Oh." I took a cleaning cloth and wiped the already clean table. The silence between us extended. Only the sound of Grandma Em's breathing filled the room. My heart echoed in my ears.

"Have you been avoiding me because of Jannette or your job?"

I didn't turn to his voice. "I didn't want to cause problems." Changing the subject was necessary. If I didn't, I'd open a door I'd kept shut for months. "Grandma Em is much quieter. Did the doctor give her something?"

"He gave her laudanum to help her sleep. He felt she might be in pain."

There was nothing left to clean.

"Jerusha, you didn't answer my question. Sit down for a moment."

I took the seat at the far side of the table. In the small cabin, I was still only feet away.

"Were you avoiding me because of your job?"

"I didn't want to cause trouble—not with you and your father, not with Jannette—and I didn't want to be sent home in disgrace. With only a few days left in the school year, I'm not concerned about my employment."

"Won't you be here next year?"

"They hired a relative of Mrs. Skidmore's. I thought you knew."

"No one told me."

"I assumed it was common knowledge."

Ammon's stomach rumbled.

I stood and went to the larder, I hadn't even collected the eggs. "Neither of us ate dinner. I'll see what I can find."

"Bread and cheese will do. I'm not very hungry."

I sliced bread and cheese. There was half of a meat pie left on the shelf in the cellar, so we ate that too.

"What will you do after the term is over?"

"Go home to Salt Lake."

"Do you have plans beyond that?"

"I might find another teaching position." Miss Cook hadn't offered me a job, but I hoped for a recommendation.

"Were you courting anyone when before you came here?"

I pushed my plate back. "A widower had asked me to marry him. He was desperate; I was not. His continued interest was enough to keep others from approaching me. He thought if he kept asking, I'd say yes. That is the primary reason I applied here. My mother writes that he is married now."

"Would you be willing to come back to our valley?"

I closed my eyes and pictured the valley at sunset from the rise. "I like it here. It wouldn't be the same without Em, and I don't know that I have the heart to fall in love with another set of students only to give them up." It wouldn't be the same without him either.

"No, it wouldn't be the same without Grandma. I wish…"

I looked up when he didn't complete the sentence. I wished so many things and most of them had been about Ammon. There was a long silence. Emotions played across his face, pain, sadness. I looked away to give him privacy.

"I wish we could have those weeks back from the fall, the three of us enjoying dinner. The weeks before my father warned me away."

"What did he tell you?" I asked.

"You were coming dangerously close to having your contract terminated. And that it would be my fault if no one ever hired you again."

"It would have taken two of us. I know of a few teachers who are engaged. They managed to finish out the year without scandal. I think your father was more worried that I wasn't from the valley."

"I wanted to dance with you at the Christmas dance."

"I'd been put in my place. I didn't even dare dance with David. I wish I had. He'll never hear music again." Tears that I had been holding back all day came then. I wasn't just crying for David or Grandma Em. I was crying for us. For a friendship we let slip away. "Pardon me."

I stood to leave. Ammon beat me to the door, simultaneously blocking my exit and giving me a place to go as he wrapped his arms around me. I wasn't sure how long we stood together sharing our grief. His own tears dropped on my head.

After a few minutes of silence, he smoothed my hair back. I hadn't even thought of it since my run. I must have looked a fright. But I wouldn't move from where I was for anything.

"Grandma told me I was being an idiot."

His words startled me as I stepped back, wiping my eyes with my damp handkerchief. "Why would she say that?"

"Because I was avoiding you." He ran his hands down my arms to my hands and back to my shoulders. "She told me God brought you to the valley for a reason and it wasn't to just teach school."

"She said something like that to me once too."

"I'm not sure what she'd think of me now."

"Why?" I tried to read the look on his face, but the lantern's circle of light left this corner of the cabin in shadows.

"Because it's inappropriate to want to kiss you while she is ill on the other side of the room."

A giggle escaped my lips. I clamped my hand over my mouth. Laughing was far worse than kissing.

Ammon hooked a finger around my wrist and pulled my hand away. His lips brushed mine. Twice. Three times. Then remained touching mine. I'd never been kissed and always wondered if I would know what to do. I gasped, and that seemed to be the right thing as his mouth moved, guiding mine. I was aware of everything and nothing at the same time. Ammon's arms holding me close. My hands found their way to the back of his neck. The wordless movement of our lips communicated volumes. We ended the kiss. I leaned my head against his chest, trying for the second time that day to find my breath.

A noise from the corner brought me back. We hurried across the room to Em's bed. Her eyes were open, and she smiled crookedly at us. "Ap-a tea?"

I put the kettle on.

Epilogue

THE TRAIN CLIMBED ITS WAY over the hill. I looked back over my shoulder, only seeing my little corner of the valley in my mind.

The children had surprised me by having David in their play. He had written in his own part. I wished Ammon and Grandma Em could have been there to watch. She'd recovered somewhat from her apoplexy and could now sit for a short period. She couldn't be left alone for very long. Ammon hired Mary to care for her during the next three weeks with the help of another woman. My visit home—no, to Salt Lake, the valley was my home now--would be brief. Only long enough to make a few preparations to return.

I didn't worry about my parents' reactions to my announcement. Mother would rally my sisters, aunts, and everyone else to sew me a wedding dress and gather items for housekeeping.

Ammon was busy fashioning a roof for his house. He would come to Salt Lake to meet my family before we returned to Logan for our wedding. We'd live with Grandma Em until the house was ready to move her up with us—a plan she protested with her half smile. Each day, she seemed stronger. If she'd regained all the strength in her right side, I might have accused her of pretending in order to play matchmaker. Understanding her slurred words took patience. Last night she asked us to open her trunk and unwrap a lace shawl.

She asked Ammon to put it around me. She wore it on her wedding day, and I will wear it on mine. When I return to the valley.

Historical Notes

OFTEN WHEN RESEARCHING FOR MY historical novels, I run across discrepancies and differing accounts of history. As a fiction writer, I sometimes add a few convenient details of my own to complete my stories. Due to variations in dates from sources I have borrowed details from the valley from 1880 to 1890 for the background of the fictional Jerusha Hardy's world.

The inspiration for Jerusha's story is the one room Green Canyon Schoolhouse. Originally located in the vicinity of 1500 North and 1200 East, the school has been preserved by the Reynold Watkins family and can be seen at the corner of 1900 North and 1200 East in North Logan. The cabin was a residence before being used as a school for two years around 1889. For a time, the cabin was used as a tack room. In 1989 Mrs. Elaine Watkins of North Logan rescued the building. During the restoration, the shelf desks that attached to the longer walls were located and reinstalled. Many thanks to Paula Watkins Scott for showing me the building and sharing her knowledge of the area.

The community of Greenville, renamed North Logan, was first farmed in 1878. Around 1885, Greenville residents started the first schools in the area as there was not enough room in the Logan Fifth Ward building to hold the children needing school.

At that time, each ward of the Church of Jesus Christ of Latter-day Saints provided their own school. There were also several schools run by other denominations scattered around the valley, including a college, the equivalent of a modern-day high school, that took boarders. Valley-wide, less than half of the students were able to attend school because there wasn't enough room. Several accounts state that classes were taught in the Mendon jail as their stone schoolhouse overflowed. Education was varied and uneven, with school years lasting as little as three months. Notes from the Cache School district in 1891 show that teachers ranged from competent to barely literate.

The Green Canyon Quarry provided stone for the Logan Tabernacle, Logan Temple and the Temple Barn, and Logan Courthouse as well as private homes and business. In 1882, the quarry stone sold for 27.5 cents per ton on a haul-your-own-stone price from the mouth of the quarry. Both of the Green Canyon quarries can be seen today. One provided blue stone and the smaller one provided red. It is unclear how long the quarries operated. Stone from the quarries is part of USU's Old Main, which started construction in 1889.

The exterior walls of the Logan Temple were originally painted a pinkish, off-white color to hide the dark, rough-hewn limestone, but the paint was allowed to weather away in the early 1900s. The bare stone can be seen on the exterior walls today.

The only real person in this story is Ida Ione Cook (21 April 1851–29 February 1924). In 1874, Miss Cook was the first principal at Brigham Young College, where she was also the first teacher. Interestingly enough, she is mentioned in the history of Utah State University and Logan High School as their first principal/president. Both schools were formed out of BYC. Prior to coming to Logan, Ida taught at the University of Deseret, now University of Utah. After leaving BYC, in 1892, she became the superintendent of Logan schools. I absolutely had to include her as in a time before most women could vote she accomplished amazing things.

The Mary Ann Routledge and Ralph Smith home was the first home built in North Logan from Green Canyon stone. Finished in March 1884, it still stands near 2200 North 1700 East. With eighteen-inch thick walls, I assume it will be standing for years to come. I based Ammon's house off of this home.

The globe out of the potbelly stove story occurred at another school in Cache Valley. The five-finger lesson is from the McGuffey Primer of the time period, however the McGuffey was not the preferred reader in the county.

I keep many of research finds on Pinterest: https://www.pinterest.com/LorinGrace1797.

For further notes on the history of the county, I suggest: A History of Cache County, by R Ross Peterson, 1997, Utah State Historical Society Cache County Council. Available on line http://www.riversimulator.org/Resources/History/UtahCounties/HistoryOfCacheCounty1996Peterson.pdf

About the Author

LORIN GRACE WAS BORN IN Colorado and has been moving around the country ever since, living in eight states and several imaginary worlds. She holds a degree in graphic design which comes in handy with creating book covers. Currently, she lives with her husband, and a dog who is insanely jealous of her laptop.

When not writing, Lorin enjoys creating graphics, visiting historical sites, museums, painting furniture, and reading. Three of her books, her debut novel, *Waking Lucy* (2017), *Mending Fences* (2018), and *Not the Bodyguard's Baby* (2020) have won Recommend Read awards in the League of Utah Writers Published book contest.

Preview of

Rescuing the Sheriff's Heart

A TRAIN WHISTLED A WARNING as the engineer released the steam brakes, obscuring the last of the well-wishers waving to loved ones. Emily's heart sped in time with the clicking of the wheels on the tracks as the departing train gained speed toward far-off places and new beginnings. Were any of the passengers bound for a fresh start, too? She clutched her chatelaine bag to still her hands. As a recent graduate of Bradford College, she must always act with utmost decorum in public. Only a half hour more and she would board one of those trains, the first step of her one-way trip to a new life and freedom.

"Emily? Emily Anne? Emily Anne Wilson?" Uncle Carl's voice brought her back from her musings.

"Sorry, Uncle, I was daydreaming."

"No need to leave before your train does." A hint of mirth tinged her uncle's voice. At least he didn't dismiss her dreams. The Civil War veteran leaned heavily on his son Percy's arm. "You have the money we gave you?"

"Yes. It is safe." Emily smiled, not wanting to tell her uncle she'd hidden the majority of her funds inside of her corset. She'd gained a healthy fear of train robbers from reading the dime novels her cousin Barbara left around the house. Thus she spent an hour sewing the five gold double eagles into the lining of her undergarment. If the coins were meant for cousin Percy's future, she didn't want them. "Your gift was so generous. Are you sure it is not too much?"

"I've been waiting years to give you something that your Aunt Melba couldn't get her hands on. Speaking of...I thought they'd be here to see you off." Her uncle shifted his cane. According to Percy, the injury his father received at Gettysburg had been giving him more trouble than usual the past few weeks. Which was why Uncle Carl missed her graduation.

"I'm sure they went to the wrong station." Percy laughed. With four railway stations in Boston, it would have been an easy mistake. However, they all assumed that wherever Uncle Harlan, Aunt Melba, and Barbara were, it would be nowhere near any of the stations.

A portly man rushed up to them, his face red from the June heat. "I made it." He puffed between each word. "Where are Melba and Barbara?"

"I thought they'd be with you, Uncle Harlan." It was the politest answer Emily could give.

"No, I've been at the bank this morning, working on the expansion of the warehouse. I told her to meet me here. After the way she—" Uncle Harlan's voice faded as he looked around.

That was probably as much of an apology as Emily would get for the snub she received from Aunt Melba at graduation last week.

"Did our girl tell you about the honors she won?" Harlan asked his brother Carl.

"Our Emily isn't one for bragging, but Percy did enough for both of them. He said Emily out shown them all in her beautiful dress and her Valedictorian speech was better than the one at his own graduation at Harvard." Uncle Carl's warm gaze was worth a dozen fatherly hugs.

She'd tried to explain the dress was nothing more than a dress left at the school nearly two decades ago and made over by a dozen charity students like her. In Texas, she'd never have to take charity again.

Percy nodded. For a moment, Emily was afraid he'd launch into his nonsense about how every man there was jealous, because Percy was Emily's escort in the absence of a father and Uncle Carl. Uncle Harlan had escorted his own daughter for the final promenade across campus.

"A fine speech it was." Uncle Harlan pulled a watch from his vest pocket and craned his neck to look around. "Something in Latin about service, I believe."

"*Surgo Ut Prosim*. I rise to serve. It is Bradford College's motto. I delivered the entire speech to Uncle Carl after dinner on Sunday. He endured it well."

Percy's mouth quirked at the inside joke. His father had cheered so loudly that a policeman walking down the street hushed him through an open window. Emily's cheeks warmed at the memory.

Uncle Carl eyed his brother. "Percy made her put on her graduation dress. Our girl is a fine seamstress. If she didn't want to be a teacher out west so badly, she could start a shop here in Boston. I wouldn't have believed it was made over if she hadn't told me."

Uncle Harlan swallowed and looked away. If they were not in a public place, Uncle Carl would likely point out other deficiencies in the care she received in the decade since her parents' passing. Although her uncle's arguments had won her some freedoms and privileges over the years, it wouldn't matter anymore.

"I'm not that good." Emily had only planned on keeping the lace she'd added to the bodice, which was all she could afford on the allowance her aunt sent to supplement her scholarship money. However, the school matron felt that after fifteen years the white dress could not handle being made over again. With white wedding dresses being all the rage, many of the graduates were planning to use their graduation gowns as a base for their wedding. Others, like Emily, were always destined to be teachers and would eventually dye the dresses a more serviceable color.

Uncle Harlan wiped his brow with his rumpled handkerchief. "I have something for you. Probably too little too late, but..." Uncle Harlan pulled four gold coins from his pocket. "Hopefully, this will help you on your journey. There isn't much of your father's money left. I'll guard the remainder for you as a kind of dowry. I thought I should give it to you now, but Melba warned me that any extra money is likely to be stolen by one of those outlaws."

With effort, Emily kept her jaw clamped shut. There was still money? Aunt Melba told her the inheritance had run out years ago. Emily slid the coins into her reticule. "Thank you, Uncle, that is extremely generous of you."

To the surprise of everyone, Aunt Melba and Barbara joined them. "There you are. I thought we would have missed the train."

Uncle Carl pulled Emily into a one-armed hug. "We were just discussing how honored Emily's parents would have been—their little girl making a speech and finishing first in Bradford's class of 1879."

Aunt Melba cleared her throat. "It's a shame Barbara didn't speak. Why, with her thespian medal, she would have charmed us all, not read scripture and discussed the future."

Bradford College had deep religious traditions. Scripture wasn't optional. A full third of the women in her graduating class were either marrying ministers or heading out as missionaries to foreign lands.

"And my dress would have looked ever so much better up on the stage, Mother." Barbara smoothed the front of a green day dress Emily had never seen before, drawing attention to the flounces. "Do you like my newest gown? I am to have luncheon with Mrs. Gray. Her son is in line to inherit the family business, you know. He paid particular attention to me after church on Sunday."

"Young Mr. Gray told my darling Barbara he hoped to see her again. All of Boston recognizes what the college regents missed when they passed over Barbara as a choice for the graduation speech." Aunt Melba fluttered her fan to bring attention to her, as the feather fan wasn't necessary yet in the morning's cool.

Dramatic didn't cover her cousin's acting skills, both on and off the stage. Emily held her tongue one last time. She'd learned years ago that contradicting her aunt always ended up unpleasantly for all. Even at school, she had to be careful about what she said lest Aunt Melba find a way to cut off the few dollars left from her inheritance after her parents died. Pointing out that Barbra's less than stellar grades were the reason she was never even considered as a representative for the graduation class may bring a momentary satisfaction. But she was her mother's daughter, not her aunt's.

A tight-lipped smile was all Emily could manage. For nine years she'd worn Barbara's cast-offs, and endured Aunt Melba's explanations about how her father had squandered his share of the business. She'd been dependent on others for too long. Emily would not be beholden to anyone for her care again.

"Oh dear, look at the time. We can't be late to your luncheon, dear. We have calls to make first." Aunt Melba rushed out of the station with Barbara in tow as the uniformed man announced the ten-minute call for Emily's train.

"Be sure to write." Uncle Harlan kissed Emily's cheek and disappeared out of the same door as Aunt Melba.

Uncle Carl wobbled on his cane.

"Father, why don't you sit down, and I'll walk Emily to her car. I am sure her friend's family is nearby." Percy led his father to a wood bench.

Emily followed and kissed her favorite uncle on the cheek. "I love you and I'll write."

Uncle Carl pressed three silver dollars into her palm. "They might help get an extra meal and a room if the train gets stuck."

"Thank you." Emily choked back the tears. She was leaving the only two people in the world who cared for her. Moving as far as Texas meant she would probably never see Uncle Carl again. "Goodbye."

Percy tugged on her elbow. "Come Emily, I believe I see your friend's family waiting near the last Pullman car."

"Of course." Emily took Percy's offered arm.

"Is our aunt always so short on praise?"

Emily carefully considered her words. She'd rarely been in both of her uncle's family's presence at the same time. An estrangement with unexplained nuances only allowed her a few days each summer with Uncle Carl and Percy. Emily never told them about life at Uncle Harlan's home. "Aunt Melba would rather I not outshine our cousin. But she has been kind enough since I am nothing but a poor orphan."

"Not poor, surely. Your father owned a third of the business."

Emily shrugged. "That was then; times are difficult now. But I had enough for my schooling." Uncle Carl would feel badly if he knew most of the funds had come from the scholarship alluded to in her speech. "Now I shall go out on my own. I dare say Aunt Melba will be relieved as she intends Barbara to wed by next spring and I would only be in the way of her prospects. I am not entirely sure she believes Texas is far enough."

Percy paused and studied her. "I'm afraid I don't comprehend your meaning. The fellow who would wish to win Barbara's hand could never interest you. Perhaps because I don't have sisters, the intricacies of your situation baffles me. Must you go so far from home for a job?"

"I found a job at a private school in Hiramsville, Texas. They teach year-round, so I can start as soon as I get there. They even sent an advance for my train tickets. I'll be teaching English and history and earn sixty dollars a month. Very few jobs offer even half as much."

"Are you sure the offer is legitimate? Texas is full of villains. Some cowboy could be trying to get you down there under false pretenses." Percy looked down at her, eyes full of concern. An older brother couldn't be more protective than her cousin. Life would have been so different had she been permitted to live with him and Uncle Carl after her parents' deaths.

"I've been exchanging letters with Mrs. B. Leblanc for almost three months now, working out the particulars. Her handwriting is too fine to be anything but a lady's. And her letters are on official letterhead."

"I worry about you." Percy's words were foreign to her ears.

A hundred "if only's" raced through her head. Before any tears could escape her eyes, Emily changed the subject. "See, there's Amanda and her family. Her fiancé is a minister near Austin. I'll be traveling with her and her old governess almost all the way. Safety in numbers."

Percy nodded. "Take care. Write often. We will worry about you." He hugged her tight. Ignoring the shocked looks of Amanda's family who likely didn't know of her relationship.

Emily hugged her cousin back. "It will all work out. I know my purpose is to teach and help others. Remember my speech, *surgo ut prosim*, I rise to serve."

The moments before sunrise hailed in the peaceful hour of the morning after the bars and bordellos closed and before the stores and respectable establishments opened. Over the past three years, mornings had become TJ's favorite time of day. That hour before the sun could attempt to do what Santa Anna hadn't done over forty years ago at the Alamo and chase the men out of Texas became his refuge from the day. TJ gathered his papers, intent on reading as he sat on the porch behind the two-and-a-half story stone jail overlooking the Brazos River. There he'd watch the eastern sky change from grays to golds to blue to remind himself that in the chaos of the day to come, God existed.

Pounding on the boardwalk chased away the silence. A dust-covered boy burst into TJ's office. "Sheriff! Sheriff! Doc Palmer says come quick!"

TJ tossed his papers back onto the desk, toppling the nameplate proclaiming him Sheriff Thomas Jefferson Morgan. So much for the quiet morning. Dr. Palmer wouldn't have sent Donny for anything other than an emergency. "Office or house?"

"His house. Ya gotta hurry. Doc says she's dying!" Donny didn't stick around to see if the sheriff followed him into the deserted street.

TJ closed the door behind him and ran the short distance to Dr. Palmer's home, cutting through backyards and alleys as Donny had. A dog barked as he sprinted past the minister's house. The doctor's chickens squawked when TJ burst through the back gate.

A lamp burned in Dr. Aidan Palmer's kitchen window. TJ hopped up on the porch and entered through the partially open door.

"Doc?"

"In here, TJ."

TJ followed his friend's voice into a small room off the kitchen. A woman, unrecognizable under the bruises and swelling to her face, lay on a narrow cot. The torn silk gown exposed a lace covered corset.

"Rose wants to talk to you." Aidan stood and whispered the next words. "She doesn't have long."

Rose? One of Belle's girls? Most of her scalp was missing. What remained of her blonde hair lay bloodied and matted. None of Mrs. Belle's girls would have been far enough out of town last night to meet up with the occasional Indian who'd escaped removal to Oklahoma. Someone had meant to throw suspicion in another direction. TJ knelt next to the cot. "Who did this to you, Rose?"

"You came. My name is Cecilia Pru…it…Belle changed… drugged…" Rose closed her eyes and dragged in a ragged breath, "deceived me. I was to teach—" She clutched TJ's hand as if holding on to a lifeline in a rushing river and gasped for breath. "Stop… tea…from Bost…on…save…" The words rattled in Rose's throat. She fell silent, her gaze fixed on the ceiling. The secret Rose tried to tell died with her.

Aidan held his stethoscope to her chest for a minute. "Sheriff, I'm sorry to say you have a murder on your hands. The only animal that would do this is a man."

The doctor's conclusion matched TJs. "She didn't say who beat her by name, did she?"

Aidan closed Rose's eyes and pulled the sheet over her head. He paused a moment before looking at TJ. "No, but we can both guess. Belle doesn't let her customers do this much damage."

It wouldn't be the first time Belle instructed her henchmen to make sure one of the doves knew her place. Not that he'd ever been able to prove it. "How did Rose get here?"

"Your guess is as good as mine. She woke all the chickens less than a half hour ago. Got to my back porch before she collapsed. I'm not sure how she found my place, she's never been here before." Doc didn't need to explain. He wasn't the kind of man that stepped foot in Belle's for non-medical reasons. "She's been repeating herself and asking for you every minute or so. I'm surprised she held on as long as she did."

"What am I supposed to prevent? Tea in Boston? I'm a hundred years too late for the Boston Tea party." TJ ran his hand through his hair. "She must have thought it very important. More important than her life." A different name? Drugged? TJ's mind whirled as he tried to put the pieces together.

"Rose kept talking about teaching and being tricked and asking for you. I think there might be someone else she wants you to save." Surely Belle had more than enough working girls she didn't need to trick more of them into the trade.

"Information that someone didn't want her to pass on. Tea could be a teacher. But Boston is so far away, it must be another town."

Aidan washed his hands in the basin on a corner washstand. "It's my fault she's dead."

TJ looked at the covered body. In his unprofessional opinion, no doctor could have saved Rose. "What do you mean?"

"In March, when Dr. Jones was out of town, they called me to Belle's for the health check on her employees. Belle wasn't happy it was me instead of Jones since I'm against legalizing the brothels. She's afraid I'll convince her ladies to leave. But to be licensed, the girls need their health checks, so she let me in. Rose had bruises on her ribs. I'd asked her about them, but her only response was to look at the ruffian Belle assigned to witness the examinations and shake her head. I asked her the normal questions about being a willing worker. Rose's answer was so carefully worded I only realized a few days ago what she'd meant when she told me, 'As willing as Briseis.' I was going to see if I could talk with her again this week."

TJ never heard of the name. "Who is Briseis?"

"A captive slave in Homer's *Iliad*, forced to become a concubine. I was rereading it last Sunday night." Aidan dried his hands, shaking his head. "I've forgotten some of my old school lessons. Two months! She asked for help two months ago and I couldn't figure it out."

"I didn't think any of Belle's girls were educated enough to have read Homer." TJ turned away to avoid looking at the body, not admitting that he never finished his reading assignments that term.

"Neither did I, but what little she told us paints a grim picture. It isn't uncommon for Belle's or Harold's girls to use opium or cocaine to dull their pain. What if Rose didn't enter the profession willingly? I only heard a bit more than you did. If I understood her, Rose—or Cecilia—found herself trapped in a world she didn't want to be in. If Belle did trick and drug her, I think you also have kidnapping on your list of charges."

"Why didn't she leave in March? She could have when you talked to her then."

Aidan paced across the room and back. "The message she gave me was so cryptic. I should have done more to figure it out. Other girls have been more direct in asking to leave. Maybe she had no place to go. What friends or family would take her back after working in a brothel? You know people's attitudes. And if she had no family, who would even come looking for her? Why didn't I try to piece it together?" He walked to the doorway and back.

"For her to use such a cryptic message, she may have been threatened. So why run now and risk death? And who am I supposed to save?"

Aidan shook his head. "I'm a doctor, not a detective. Why don't I tell you what I can from an examination? Then I'll send Donny for the undertaker."

"Better hurry. I don't want the whole town gawking."

"No great mystery about how she died." Aidan uncovered one limb at a time, cataloging the injuries. "Some of these bruises are older than tonight. Look at their color. It's a wonder she made it to my backyard on this ankle. It's been twisted for a while. Oh… what do we have here?" He extracted a bit of crumpled paper from the dead woman's fist and handed it to TJ.

"Looks like part of a telegram." The paper had more blood than ink on it.

THE WESTERN UN—
Received advan—
Arrive Jun—
Teac—

TJ turned the paper over. "The cable originated in 'Massa—' so the 'Bost' Rose mentioned could be Boston after all. Not much to go on, is it? Could Belle be offering women teaching jobs and tricking or drugging them into her service? Belle claims that the best come begging to work for her and she turns them away. How am I supposed to find a teacher when I don't know what she looks like or when she is coming?"

"A woman from Massachusetts in Hiramsville will stand out like a hot-house flower in a field of bluebonnets."

"I'll have Donny watch the Fort Worth and Rio Grande trains for the next few weeks. Someone from that far away would change lines in Dallas. Belle will send someone to meet who-ever is coming."

"Pay Donny well if he is watching the station as he won't be doing as many errands." A grin lit the doctor's face.

"It's my privilege to keep the kid employed." Not a hardship. They'd been seeing to Donny's family's welfare by keeping him honestly employed.

Aidan covered the body again. "I'm sure he will still find work with me. If I hadn't delivered him myself, I would think he was twins or even triplets. He is always around when I need him, but then I see him working for Henry's store, delivering things or running for you just as often."

"He is a hard worker. I gave him a dime last week, and he told me I overpaid him. Swept off the walk for free the next day. There are only two trains a day from Fort Worth. It won't take all his time."

TJ walked home the long way on streets filled with men going about their business and children anxious to play before their mothers called them in from the heat. Trouble was coming. He felt it in his bones, sure as Old Man Whitaker knew when a tornado was brewing.

For retailers see LorinGrace.com